# BRING ME WILD HORSES

Center Point
Large Print

Also by Chuck Martin and available from Center Point Large Print:

*Sixgun Town*
*Hell-Bender from Texas*
*Gun-Boss Reynolds*

# BRING ME WILD HORSES

## CHUCK MARTIN

CENTER POINT LARGE PRINT
THORNDIKE, MAINE

This Center Point Large Print edition
is published in the year 2024 by arrangement with
Golden West Inc.

Copyright © 1951 by Phoenix Press.

All rights reserved.

Originally published in the US by Phoenix Press.

The text of this Large Print edition is unabridged.
In other aspects, this book may vary
from the original edition.
Printed in the United States of America
on permanent paper sourced using
environmentally responsible foresting methods.
Set in 16-point Times New Roman type.

ISBN: 979-8-89164-308-6

The Library of Congress has cataloged this record
under Library of Congress Control Number: 2024940284

# BRING ME WILD HORSES

# CHAPTER ONE
## HORSE TAMER

Crag Tinsley was the law in Lanthrope, Texas. The city marshal was a big man with wide powerful shoulders, and a jaw like a granite crag. An unlighted black cigar usually was clenched tightly between his strong teeth at the left side of his firm, generous mouth. Tinsley seldom found it necessary to resort to the Colt .45 six-shooter thonged low on his right leg, but it was evident at a glance that here was a peace officer who was both fast and deadly with the tools of his trade.

The town was filled with horse-traders who had gathered for the monthly auction. The corrals of the auctioneer, "Dapper Jim" Stacey, were filled with horses of every size and breeding, and Stacey was getting ready to open the sale. Crag Tinsley was watching the auctioneer with a steady, unwinking stare.

Dapper Jim knew horses and the men who trafficked in horse-flesh. He was a tall slender man who wore the only riding breeches in Lanthrope, English riding boots, and a derby hat. He was never seen without the long buggy whip which was as much a part of him as the loud checkered coat with rounded cut-away tails.

Jim Stacey was honest, because he worked for a straight five percent, cash on the barrel-head.

"Howdy, Crag!" he called to the marshal, waving a sheath of papers in his left hand. "It's a fine bright Texas day, if you was to ask me."

"Which I didn't," Tinsley grunted ungraciously, and shifted the black cigar in his mouth.

Then he stiffened and turned his head toward the north end of the main street as though to listen. His eyes narrowed as a frown puckered his weathered brow. A strange sound was intruding among the customary noises of the busy street. Dapper Jim Stacey heard it also, and walked swiftly across the sales ring to stand near Tinsley.

"Sounds like a drum," Stacey murmured, "but the war between the States has been done and finished for more'n ten years. It is a drum, or I don't know hosses!"

Crag Tinsley was staring up the street, with his Stetson pulled low over his eyes. He shifted the cigar again between his lips, spat from the corner of his mouth, and took a deep breath.

"I've seen most everything, but get a look at this," he muttered hoarsely. "There's a law against loose hosses on the streets in this town, and this hombre must be a stranger."

The two men stared as the rhythmic beat of the drum grew louder, and they didn't believe what they saw. A man was walking down the middle of the wide dirt street, dressed in tailored grey whipcord, and he was beating a drum which hung from the back of his neck by a lanyard. The stranger's polished boots twinkled in the bright morning sun, but he looked neither to the right nor to the left as he beat the tight skin with an ever-changing series of fancy rolls.

The drum was an attention-getter but the crowds following the drummer on both plank sidewalks were more interested in what was following the well-dressed drummer. A sleek black stallion was curveting and prancing several paces behind the drummer, and there was no sign of trapping on the big horse except for a light head-stall from which a short, looped thong dangled.

"What a hoss!" Jim Stacey murmured in a low humming voice. "That stud must be all of sixteen hands high, and mostly thoroughbred. He follows that skin-beater like a dog, and he's going to bust up my sale from the looks of things!"

Crag Tinsley frowned as his rugged face grew hard with the reflection of vested authority. His eyes held to the stranger who was now about twenty-five yards away from the auction corrals. Tinsley was making a silent inventory as he checked off the drummer's points.

The man with the talking drum would be about thirty years old. He had piercing black eyes, and hair of the same hue. His face was thin, but strongly moulded, and smoothly shaven. He seemed perfectly poised and confident. Here was a man who knew where he was going, and what he was going to do after he got there.

Wide shoulders sloping down to narrow hips, told a story of a saddle-athlete. Tinsley stared at the swelling chest, but it was the stranger's long-fingered hands which fascinated the marshal. Slender delicate hands which the officer knew were possessed of amazing strength.

Crag Tinsley was about to step out to halt the drummer and his prancing stallion when the stranger swerved sharply and came directly toward the big entrance of the horse yard. A double roll of the drums came to an abrupt end which left the ears tingling and straining for the rataplan to begin again. But the stranger stopped and bowed slightly from the hips as he addressed both the marshal and Dapper Jim Stacey.

"Allow me to present myself," he said in a low, smooth voice. "I am Centaur King, and my stallion is Major Domo. I have brought the crowds to your auction sale, and I ask only for the opportunity to make a brief talk after the sale has been completed!"

"Centaur King, eh?" Tinsley repeated, and shifted his unlighted cigar. "Never heard of you or yore Major Domo hoss, but you're under arrest. There's a City Ordinance against loose hosses on the streets of Lanthrope."

"Loose horse?" the stranger echoed, and the trace of a smile curved his full red lips. "But I have no loose horse on the streets of your busy and thriving town."

"Well, I'll be hanged!" Crag Tinsley spat out, as his eyes raised to stare at the black stallion.

The big stallion was standing just behind King, as though tied to a post. The loop of the rawhide thong circled the stallion's right leg, and the only movement was the twitching of the sleek hide as the horse dislodged a blue bottle fly. Centaur King spoke to Dapper Jim Stacey in flattering recognition as one of the craft.

"Flick your whip and tell Major Domo to get into the yard, Mr. Stacey."

"You know my name?" Stacey asked, and a pleased smile spread across his tanned features. "You, Major!" he said quietly. "Into the yard with you!"

Stacey stepped to one side and flicked his whip lightly. Only the silken lash caressed the flank of the big horse, but the stallion made no move to obey. The auctioneer repeated his order and flicked his whip again, but the stallion did not move.

"Ah, yes, I am forgetful," Centaur King apologized softly. "Pardon me while I untie him." Leaning over he took the rawhide thong in his left hand. The stallion gracefully raised his hoof, and King removed the loop. "Now tell him again," Centaur King said to Dapper Jim Stacey.

Stacey stared like a man who is seeing magic

performed. He flicked his whip lightly, and now he spoke more sharply.

"You, Major Domo. Get inside the yard pronto!"

The big horse raised its head proudly and obeyed without hesitation. He circled and came up behind Stacey, resting his velvety muzzle on the auctioneer's right shoulder. Stacey smiled and offered his right hand to King.

"I remember hearing about you, Centaur King," he said cordially. "Welcome to Lanthrope and my auction. Yes, I remember you well now. You're a hoss tamer!"

"Yes," King answered with simple dignity. "I have the gift!"

Crag Tinsley frowned as he watched and listened. The play had been taken completely away from the law, and the marshal resented the manner in which it had been accomplished.

"Gift?" Tinsley broke in roughly. "What gift, if the Law might be so bold as to ask?"

"Centaur King, let me introduce you to Crag Tinsley, our fearless and respected city marshal," Stacey said quickly. "Crag, Mr. King can tame a wild hoss by touching the beast, and talking to it. There's work a plenty for him in and around Lanthrope, and I for one, want to see him work his magic!"

"Howdy, King," Tinsley growled softly, and with a trace of suspicion in his gruff voice. "Now

12

me, I don't hold with this magic business, and you might as well know it."

"Perhaps I can show you how I work at my calling," King answered with a smile. "Seeing is believing."

"We've got some of the best bronc-riders in the west, right here in Lanthrope," Tinsley argued stubbornly. "There never was a hoss what couldn't be rode, and they never was a cowboy what couldn't be throwed."

"But I'm not a bronc-stomper," King said with quiet dignity. "My work starts after these other men give up."

Crag Tinsley stepped back and studied King for a long moment. It was plain that the marshal thought the stranger was hoorawing him, and he said so.

"I wouldn't hooraw a man," Centaur King said gravely. "I know what I can do, and I've worked at it for years."

"Yeah, well there's work a plenty breaking out the big green ones in these parts," Tinsley answered gruffly. "You aiming to get you a job on a cattle-spread, or buck 'em out by the contract?"

Centaur King's eyes held a far-away look. He paused before answering the marshal, and then his voice was that of a dreamer.

"I never stay long in one place, Tinsley. I'm looking for something, and some day I might find the right place."

"Or the right girl," Tinsley said dryly. "Nothing like a wife and a home to cure a feller of the itching heel."

"You might be right," King agreed without interest. "I like to travel."

"You'll stay a while in Lanthrope, won't you, King?" Jim Stacey interrupted.

As he spoke, a terrific hubbub came from one of the crowded holding corrals behind the show ring. Horses were rearing and plunging madly, striking at each other, and kicking out with wicked heels. Several hostlers were trying to quiet the fighting animals, but the noise only increased in fury as the fight became general.

"I'll have several scarred hosses," Jim Stacey worried, as he watched the fight.

"With your permission," Centaur King said quietly, but he wasted no time waiting for an answer.

King moved swiftly, took the rawhide thong, and the big stallion raised its right hoof. King passed the loop over the hoof, walked swiftly across the ring toward the corral, and the big stallion watched with bright eyes, but did not follow.

Centaur King climbed the high bar stockade and jumped down into the corral between two range stallions. They were rearing high and clawing at each other while they screamed their rage. Centaur King looked like a boy between the two whistling range monarchs, but he did not give back a step. He spoke softly in a low authoritative manner.

"Down horse! Get back, boy!"

The maddened stallions lunged at each other, and only the pricking forward of small eyes gave evidence that they heard that commanding voice. Moving in swiftly, King slapped first one stallion and then the other with the flat of his hand. His voice was more incisive when he spoke again.

"Back, I say!"

The hooves of a big grey swerved over King's head, then thudded down several inches to the right. The other stallion stopped a whistling scream and dropped its front hooves at the same time. Centaur King smiled gently and slapped the horse lightly on the neck.

The two big stallions backed away, sniffing at this audacious man-thing who had dared to jump between their striking hooves. Centaur King was speaking softly, then he was moving between other fighting horses which were kicking and lunging at each other.

"Down, I say!" his low voice commanded imperatively, but it was the stern voice of one who is accustomed to being obeyed without question.

The gaping hostlers stared in amazement, too stunned for speech. Centaur King was walking slowly among the milling horses, speaking softly, and placing his long-fingered hands here and there on a quivering flank. And at his touch, each animal became docile and quiet.

Dapper Jim Stacey watched and put out a hand to restrain Crag Tinsley who was moving toward the corral.

"Don't interfere, Crag," Stacey warned. "He won't get hurt if we keep away, but we are watching something most men only hear about, and few of them believe. Centaur King has the gift!"

"Gift," Tinsley growled. "What in time is this gift you keep yammering about as though it was some kind of a treasure?"

"It is a treasure, and I wish to heaven I had it," Stacey answered in a whisper. "Mighty few men ever have it, and sometimes a hundred years goes by without any man having this gift. It's the touch of a hand a hoss recognizes, and something in the voice. Centaur King is a master with hosses—with any hoss!"

"Now look, Dapper," Tinsley protested. "I've heard plenty of tall tales, and the windies these here cowhands spin. But don't expect me to swallow this yarn about that feller having power over hosses, wild or tame. He ain't more'n five-feet-nine, and it would crowd him to tip the beam at a hundred and fifty pounds!"

"The crowd is all here, thanks to Centaur King," Stacey answered evasively. "I'm going to ask him to talk to the traders before the auction begins. You listen close to what he says, Crag. You might learn something about this gift I was telling you about."

Centaur King was climbing the bars and coming out of the crowded corral. He smiled slowly at Stacey, washed his hands in a horse trough, then bowed slightly.

"Some of those critters would have been crippled," he said to Stacey. "I hope you don't mind my interference."

"Mind it?" Stacey murmured. "We owe you a debt, Centaur King. My auction begins in five minutes, and I suggest that you talk some to the traders before I start. It's the least we can do for what you've done for us."

"It was nothing," King answered with a shrug. "Call for me when you want me to speak."

"What did you do to those first two stallions?" Stacey asked humbly. "They would have killed each other."

"I just spoke to them in their own language," King answered modestly, but his manner was sincere. "I just laid my hands on them, and they became quiet."

"You never use a whip?"

"Very seldom," King answered. "Sometimes it is necessary the first time if a horse has eaten loco weed."

"We kill that kind off," Stacey stated bluntly.

"They go crazy, and they can't ever be trusted!"

"Major Domo ate loco weed," King answered quietly. "He was a killer, but now a little child can handle him. Look yonder!"

Dapper Jim turned to follow the gesture King made with his chin. He drew a deep breath, then stared at a little girl who was walking under the body of the great black stallion.

"That's Madeline, Crag Tinsley's little girl!" Stacey gasped. "She'll be killed!"

"Easy," King warned, and he smiled as he spoke gently across the yard to the big horse. "Quiet, Major. Stand perfectly still, boy!"

Crag Tinsley covered his eyes with a brawny arm. The crowd of horse traders watched without making a sound. The big horse stood without moving a muscle, even when the child stood under his belly, holding on to one front leg with a dimpled chubby hand.

"Easy, Major," King said soothingly. "You, Madeline, darlin'," he called softly. "Come here and see my pretty watch, and hear the little bells inside."

The little girl chortled happily and ran to Centaur King with her arms outstretched. He picked her up, kissed the top of her head, and pulled a fine watch from his pocket. Then he turned a knob and held the timepiece to Madeline's ear.

"Listen to the little bells," he whispered.

"Like fairy bells," the little girl said, and her eyes were round with wonder. "I like you, horsey-man."

King hugged the child and handed her to Crag Tinsley. The marshal could only gulp for a moment as he winked the scalding tears from his fierce blue eyes.

"You've got the gift, King," he said in a husky whisper. "And the whole cussed town is yores for the asking!"

Centaur King smiled when the marshal gripped his hand like a vice, but he returned the pressure until Tinsley winced.

"It's a good town," King said heartily. "And I'm in love with your daughter."

"Every no-good cowhand loves Madeline, just like all the leading citizens do," Tinsley said proudly. "I won't be forgetting this day, hoss tamer!"

Centaur King turned when Jim Stacey touched his arm. Dapper Jim introduced King, telling the crowd that he would speak briefly before the auction began. King studied the eager faces for a long moment.

"I have a knack of gentling wild and vicious horses," King began quietly, and without bravado. "For a nominal fee, I will break and gentle your worst horses, or return your money. I ask only one favour, gentlemen. Give me a chance to prove what sounds to you like a boast."

"Name the favour, Centaur King," Dapper Jim spoke up clearly. "What can we do for you?"

Centaur King smiled and held out his long-fingered hands. Expressive hands which men claimed held . . . the gift. His voice was quiet when he answered.

"Bring me the worst ones you have, gentlemen. Bring me wild horses!"

# CHAPTER TWO
## THE GOLDEN KILLER

Dapper Jim Stacey stood on a raised platform surrounded by a light rail. This was his auction block, and it occupied the centre of the show ring. With the long whip in his right hand, his lists in his left, Stacey addressed the crowd with what was known as "the patter of the feed-trough."

Stacey left little to chance, and he usually knew the horses he was selling. Tough little Texas mustangs brought ten dollars a head in the rough, and sold in strings of ten or a dozen. They would be broken later by the bronc-riders on the cattle-spreads which bought them, which meant they would be ridden into the ground four or five times, then turned over to the working cowboys as broken for cow work.

Huge draft horses went on the block—Clydesdales and Percherons, Belgians and Shires. These animals brought as high as two hundred dollars each, and were noted for their docility. Sales were brisk for the first hour when the horses were sold in lots, but the real bidding began when Stacey began to ask for bids on individual animals of proven breeding.

Centaur King had disappeared with his black

stallion, but Stacey saw the horse tamer talking to Marshal Crag Tinsley under a cottonwood tree at the far east end. A covered Conestoga wagon was also drawn up under the trees, and the team which had pulled the wagon was being fed and groomed by a half-grown boy.

"Who's the button?" the marshal asked King, indicating the boy with a thrust of his chin. "He seems kind of puny for a lad his age and size. About sixteen, I'd make a guess."

"Peg is stronger than you'd think," King told Tinsley. "He's closer to seventeen, and he adopted me down in Indian Territory several months ago. Smart lad he is, and he has a rare way with horses."

"That's a queer name, Peg," Tinsley said thoughtfully. "I knew a man once with that handle, but he had a wooden leg."

"The boy's right name is Pegasus," King explained. "Pegasus Bronte, and his family lives back in Virginia. Quality folks they are, and Pegasus means a winged horse. Don't twit the lad about his name, Marshal."

"Well, I do know," Tinsley murmured, and then he fixed King with a direct stare. "You've got a right unusual name yourself, King," he commented. "You mind telling me what 'Centaur' stands for?"

Centaur King smiled as he took a tiny vial from a coat pocket. He poured a drop of colourless liquid in one palm, returned the vial to his pocket, and massaged his palms together.

"A Centaur was a critter away back when the world was young," he explained courteously. "It was supposed to be half man and half horse, and my father liked the sound of it. I was born and raised down in Kentucky where you will find a lot of unusual names."

"I reckon," Tinsley grunted. "As well as fast hosses and beautiful women." He was watching King, who was rubbing his hands together. "If I might be so bold, what was that stuff you just put on your hands?"

"Oh, just a drop of oil," King answered carelessly. "It has no taste or odour, but it is good for the skin. Shall we go over and watch the auction? I see they are selling individual animals now."

Tinsley nodded and accompanied the horse tamer to the fringe of the crowd. The sales ring had been cleared except for Dapper Jim who stood on his platform watching three of his wranglers as they struggled with a great golden horse. A tall cattleman with longhorn moustaches called a warning.

"Mind out for El Caballo Oro!" he shouted. "He's a killer, for all his beauty!"

"That's a good name for the stallion," Tinsley remarked to King. "It means 'the golden hoss,' and he shore is one!"

"Yeah, I speak some Spanish," King replied. "I

liked the way you called my black stud, Major Domo."

"*Meyer* Domo," Tinsley repeated the Spanish pronunciation. "You Southerners all take quick to this Border Spanish we use down this way."

Centaur King was watching the struggle as the three hostlers tried to drag the big stallion into the ring. No halter fired the tossing head, but two lariats had evidently snared the regal horse to choke him down. A bull-whacker snapped his bull-whip at the stallion's flanks, and the big animal surged into the ring with a shrill scream of rage.

One of the hostlers stumbled and fell to his knees. The stallion was on top of him like a cat striking out with his right fore foot. The blow struck the prostrate man on the shoulder and knocked him flat and the other two hostlers were dragged on the ends of their ropes.

"Roll!" the moustached cattleman shouted. "Roll before he tromps you to death!"

But the man on the ground was stunned and helpless. The golden stallion reared high with front feet chopping. A gasp went up from the crowd, and the stallion's owner drew a six-shooter from the open holster on his long right leg. Then a quiet vibrant voice hummed across the sales ring.

"Down boy! Back, I say!"

The golden stallion paused for a second as the

voice penetrated even his rage. Centaur King had leaped the fence lightly, and now he was facing the big horse with both hands held up as though to push the maddened animal away from its victim.

"Back, I say!"

The cattleman held his shot, with his thumb on the hammer of his heavy six-shooter. The stallion swerved aside and thudded to the ground, missing the stunned hostler by inches. King began to talk softly, though none could understand what he was saying.

The stallion slid to a stop and reared high above the fearless horse tamer. Centaur King continued to talk, without moving. His left hand made a little outward gesture of command, and the stallion dropped his front feet to the dust, brushing King with his muscled left shoulder.

Centaur King shrugged, without moving his polished boots. His right hand raised slowly and touched the stallion lightly on the muzzle. Great snapping teeth missed that outstretched hand by a fraction of an inch, but the hand did not tremble.

A low murmur whispered from Centaur King's lips, and the stallion stopped trembling. The great arched neck lowered slightly as the stallion reached out and sniffed suspiciously at the horse tamer's hand.

Centaur King remained immovable, and not a sound came from the spell-bound crowd. The stallion's lips reached King's hand, muzzled it a time or two, and King moved his hand and stroked the sleek golden neck. Then he spoke so all could hear and understand what he said.

"Back, I say! Step back, Caballo!"

The golden stallion stiffened, then obeyed meekly. One step, another, with Centaur King following him slowly and forcing the big horse to obey his will. The horse seemed to be watching King's face which was a mixture of love and dominance.

Once more King began to talk softly to the horse in a mumble the crowd could not understand. But the great horse seemed to understand every word, and obeyed without question. Here was the Master whose word was law, and the horse seemed to be entirely under the control of that fearless man-thing who spoke a language the stallion could understand.

Centaur King reached up slowly and removed the two lariats from the great arched neck. These he threw behind him and into the crowd. Then King stooped and picked up the right forefoot while the stallion muzzled his drooping shoulder. King dropped the hoof, and picked up the left, talking all the while to the quieted horse.

Jim Stacey watched with his breath caught in his lungs as King moved back to the rear legs. But King continued to mumble softly while his hands pressed the muscled flanks. Then those hands passed down along the great tendons to the fetlock, picked up a rear hoof, and inspected the frog. Keeping close to the tail, King walked behind the stallion, picked up the other hoof, and pried a small rock from the tender frog.

His inspection finished, Centaur King straightened up and turned his back. He walked slowly to the centre of the ring without glancing back, and without speaking. The golden stallion followed him like a big, disciplined dog, and Dapper Jim Stacey took his cue as King nodded at him.

"You see before you the most beautiful hoss in all Texas," Stacey began his sales build-up. "Down here we call this kind of a horse a claybank, but over in California they call 'em palominos. The name comes from the colour more'n from the breed. A good 'un has a white mane and tail, and there's a rumour to the effect that these golden hosses are descendants of those brought over here by Cortez from Spain way back in the sixteenth century."

He paused a moment to let the historical point sink in. Centaur King was watching the big stallion, and Stacey went on with his patter.

"Joe Crawford snared this here stallion when he was a yearlin'. I mean the stallion. Sixteen hands high, four years old, and as wild as Nature. He's sound in wind and limb, with the endurance of a Spanish Barb or an Arabian, and take your choice. Gentlemen, what am I bid for this magnificent stallion, El Caballo Oro, the golden hoss?"

"One hundred dollars!" a trader called out. "He ain't fitten for nothin' but rodeos!"

"Two hundred," another man raised the bid. "I'll keep him for the stud if I can get him home!"

"Three hundred dollars!" a clear boyish voice broke in. "I'll break him for my own personal horse!"

Every man in the crowd turned to stare at the slight, half-grown boy who had crawled between the bars of the sales ring. Not more than five-feet-four, and weighing perhaps a hundred and twenty pounds. He held a canvas sack in his left hand. It clinked musically when he shook it gently to prove the sincerity of his offer.

"Ho!" the first bidder roared, a big rough man of forty-odd. "The button wants El Caballo Oro for his personal mount!"

Centaur King turned his head slightly and smiled at Pegasus Bronte. Neither said a word, but King nodded ever so slightly. These two also spoke a silent language they alone could understand.

"Three hundred!" Jim Stacey called the bid. "Do I hear four hundred?"

"He'll kill the button," Joe Crawford growled uneasily. "They ain't but one man in the world can handle that golden stud!"

Pegasus Bronte waited and listened with an

expectant fear on his thin sensitive face. He listened for another bid, and then the auctioneer spoke again. Spoke in a hurried voice as though he sensed the boy's desire, and wanted him to have his wish.

"Three hundred I'm bid," Stacey announced. "Going once, going twice . . . Gone! Sold to the button on my right, with the sack of gold in his hand, which I'll take in payment for the golden hoss. Right this way, button!"

Pegasus Bronte walked across the ring, a queer shambling figure in white riding breeches, small jockey boots, and a dinky hat on his tousled brown hair. He dumped the contents of the sack on the little shelf in front of Jim Stacey, watching while the auctioneer counted out the golden discs.

"Exactly right," Stacey commented. "You can lead your purchase from the ring, young man."

Jim Stacey had seen that look which had passed between Centaur King and Pegasus Bronte. The auctioneer knew that if the boy was with King, he'd know how to handle horses.

Centaur King did a strange thing then. He turned his back on the golden stallion, walked to the rails, and climbed through. The crowd watched the horse tamer, then turned to study the boy who had bought the stallion. Those closest to the rail began to move back.

Dapper Jim Stacey wet his lips with a tongue

which had gone suddenly dry. Big Joe Crawford began to mutter to himself as he again loosened the heavy six-shooter in his holster. The injured hostler had been helped from the ring while King had the horse under control, and Pegasus Bronte was alone with his purchase.

In a land where tall men are common, the slight figure of Pegasus Bronte seemed even more puny beside the big horse. The boy began to speak below his breath as he faced the golden stallion. For a moment he talked, and then he extended his left hand.

Back went the stallion's head with lips skinned away from his great snapping teeth. Pegasus Bronte took one step forward, talking all the while. He stooped suddenly and placed a hand on the stallion's right fore-foot. Grasping the fetlock firmly, he picked up the big foot.

The golden stallion jerked his foot away and reared high in the air. The boy ran under the chopping feet, and slapped the stallion smartly on the chest with the flat of his hand. Then he stood still and mumbled softly, just above his breath. While outside the rail, Centaur King watched and slowed down his breathing.

King told himself that Pegasus had a way with horses, but the . . . *gift* . . . was something rarely given to a man. Could it have happened more than once in a lifetime? Then King smiled confidently.

The stallion thundered to earth, missing the boy by the slightest of margins. Pegasus Bronte slapped the horse again, this time on the arched neck, and once more he held out his right hand.

Joe Crawford moaned softly, and closed his eyes, Dapper Jim Stacey leaned forward with elbows on the little shelf. But on the face of Pegasus Bronte there shone a light of confidence, and the reflection of a great love.

The golden stallion took a mincing step forward and muzzled the boy's hand gently. Pegasus gulped, recovered his poise, and spoke clearly so that all could hear what he said.

"You all pay some mind to me when I talks to you, Gold 'Un," he said, and slapped the horse gently on the chest. "You go to gettin' uppity with me, I'll knock yore dad-durned ears down!"

The great horse whickered softly and took a little step forward. Then he rested his big muzzle on the boy's slight shoulder and sighed deeply. Pegasus Bronte winked his brown eyes rapidly, and his hands went up to caress the killer horse.

"I fell in love with you the very minute I laid eyes on you, Sugar Foots," he drawled softly, in the patois of the deep south. "Now you-uns stand while I fits a riggin' on you. You go givin' me grief in front of all these folks, I aim to make you hard to find. You hear me, Gold 'Un?"

The golden stallion whickered softly in answer, and Pegasus Bronte stepped back. From inside his light jacket he took a rawhide head-stall attached to a short looped thong. The crowd watched with silent wonder as the boy stepped up to the big horse. It was impossible for him to reach the stallion's head, but Pegasus shaped his head-stall with his small hands and spoke gently to the tall horse.

"Fitten yore head down this away where I can reach you, Gold 'Un. And I don't aim to tell you but one time. You hear me, Suh?"

Jim Stacey stopped breathing for a moment, then he shook his head slowly from side to side. The great golden stallion obediently lowered its head, and the boy slipped the head-stall over the horse's nose and behind the dainty ears. Then Pegasus dropped the thong, walked around the horse, and picked up both hind legs to examine the hoofs and frogs.

That was the way with a horse, Centaur King had taught him. Make them pick up their front feet first, and you have started the first lesson of discipline. Make them step back and come forward, and when you lay hand to a horse, make sure that hand is not trembling.

The crowd watched while Pegasus examined the hind feet, running his sensitive fingers across the taut tendons.

"Good feet and stout pasterns," the crowd heard him mutter. "When I get him tucked up some in the flanks, Gold 'Un ought to win me some money in cowboy races. Built for a fast start, with plenty of bottom for the long pulls. Yes, Suh, he'll do to take along, this shere El Caballo Oro!"

Pegasus Bronte nodded his tousled head confidently as he dreamed his boyish dreams aloud. He took the rawhide thong in his left hand and turned his back. Then he walked from the ring leading his purchase, and El Caballo Oro followed him like a great docile dog, and the golden stallion's eyes were soft with worship.

Centaur King watched with an indescribable feeling tugging at his heart. He knew the great courage of his protégé, but the memory of the stallion's attack on the stumbling hostler was still fresh in King's mind.

"Oh, that was cruel," a feminine voice said behind King, and he turned very slowly to meet a pair of brown eyes which accused him even more that the girl's words.

Centaur King removed his hat and studied the girl. She was tall and slender, but superbly made. She wore leather divided skirts, a white silk blouse caught at the throat with a blue neckerchief, and cowboy boots. Her silky brown hair was caught under a creamy Stetson, and full red lips pouted at King as she faced him with just a touch of scorn.

"I beg your pardon, Miss," King said evenly. "I am Centaur King, a wandering horse tamer."

"I know," the girl said coldly. "I saw you work. You had no right to jeopardize the life of that boy!"

"You are a horse tamer?" King asked softly, but his eyes smiled at the girl.

"I love horses," the girl answered tartly, and then her face softened. "That golden stallion," she whispered. "I wanted to put my arms around his neck, but he drove me away with snapping teeth."

"You didn't love him enough," King answered bluntly. "Not nearly as much as Pegasus does."

"The superiority of man," the girl retorted.

"The superiority of love," King corrected. "And perfect love casteth out all fear!"

He turned abruptly when the girl's lip curled slightly. A hand touched his arm, and King whirled to face Dapper Jim Stacey.

"Allow me," the auctioneer said quickly. "Miss Carol Tinsley, may I present Centaur King from Kentucky?"

"How do you do?" the girl acknowledged the introduction.

"Tinsley," King repeated. "Are you related to the city marshal?"

"Slightly," the girl answered. "He is my brother."

"Then I'm glad to know you," King said cordially.

"Centaur is in love with Madeline." Stacey

tried to ease the tension, and he told Carol about the rescue of her brother's child.

Carol Tinsley flushed and extended her hand to Centaur King. "Can you forgive my rudeness?" she pleaded. "If anything had happened to Madeline . . . ?"

"Nothing did; nothing could," King replied, as he took her hand. "You see, Madeline loved Major Domo, and he knew it."

"But the Golden killer," Carol said with a shudder. "That big horse didn't love this boy you call Pegasus."

"He did," King corrected gently. "But every wild spirit is like that. Every horse is looking for one master, but sometimes they never get together. Then the horse becomes an outlaw."

"I have learned so very much in such a short time, and I feel very humble," Carol Tinsley murmured. "That boy did something I have wanted to do for more than a year."

"Perhaps he too has the gift," King said slowly. "It has been a pleasure to meet you, Miss Carol. Now if you will excuse me, I will go to help Pegasus with his treasure."

# CHAPTER THREE
## MIDNIGHT VISITOR

Pegasus Bronte reluctantly left the small corral where he had penned the golden stallion. The gear would have to be looked after for the next day's work, and Pegasus always held up his end in the unspoken partnership between himself and the man he worshipped more than anything he had ever known.

Centaur King was humming softly as he coiled ropes and adjusted hobbles. After several months' association with King, Pegasus Bronte knew little about the horse tamer except those things which pertained to their work. They both spoke the soft caressing drawl of the south, but most of their conversation was about horses.

"You all like rabbit stew for supper, Centaur?" Pegasus asked anxiously. "I knocked over a pair of cottontails with the scattergun this morning, and I done got 'em skun out and in the pot."

"Just what I need to build me up where I'm all tore down," King answered with a smile, and in his dark eyes was a deep affection for the boy who had half-crawled into his camp down in Indian Territory during a howling storm. "And how about some corn pone or shovel cake?"

"Shovel cake with pot licker on the side," the

boy answered happily. "How did you know, pard?"

Centaur King turned his face to hide the smile. "I'm a detective," King answered gravely. "I saw you scouring that shovel with clean sand, and you got a deep fire of coals yonder in that hole you dug out."

"This shere Gold 'Un, Centaur," Pegasus said gravely. "You reckon that rascal really cottons to me?"

"Peg, my lad, you handled him like an old-timer," King praised quietly. "You didn't crowd him none to put the hand again his flesh, neither did you give way an inch when he bared his teeth. You didn't shake the tiniest bit."

"Yes, Suh," Pegasus agreed gratefully. "You mind the time I pulled my hand back off that knothead down Fort Smith way? That 'un got to me with his teeth, but I learned my lesson."

Centaur King shuddered slightly. He remembered the incident too well. The horse had eaten of the poisonous loco weed, and had sensed that Pegasus Bronte was afraid of him. The bite on the boy's hand had not been severe, but it had given Centaur King a bad half hour. That had also been one of the few times he had laid the heavy whip to a killer horse. And had then ridden the savage beast into the ground in a test of mastery.

"I rode that jughead the next day," Pegasus drew on his memory. "After you got through

38

working him over, any little old gal-chip could have topped him off."

Centaur King glanced up when boots scuffed a warning. Carol Tinsley and her brother were coming up to the wagon, and the city marshal was smiling at Peg Bronte. He even called the boy by name, and Peg answered with a smile of happiness at being remembered. The smile fled from his thin face when he saw the marshal's sister.

"I want you to meet my sister, Carol, Peg," Tinsley spoke heartily. "Carol is an artist, and she wanted to make some sketches. With your permission, of course," he added hastily, as Pegasus turned away.

"I wanted to tell you how fine you looked taming that golden killer," Carol added, but Peg shrugged a thin shoulder.

"I don't want no truck with women," Pegasus said rudely. "Me nor Centaur neither one!"

"But I'm only a girl," Carol answered with a little laugh. "Surely you are not afraid of a girl."

"No'm, but I don't trust 'em none," Pegasus said bluntly.

"We don't have bad manners in this camp, Peg," Centaur King reminded the boy. "You'll do the needful, pard?"

Pegasus Bronte opened his mouth, stared at King, and then trapped his lips together. He turned to face Carol Tinsley, removed his dinky hat, and bowed from the hips.

"Sayin' I'm sorry for bein' onmannerly, Miss Carol, Ma'am," he made grudging apology. "Will you sit a spell and have a bite with we-uns?"

Crag Tinsley listened and started to smile. Peg Bronte's face darkened, but the marshal quickly corrected his mistake.

"Man, oh, man," Tinsley murmured. "Just smell that rabbit stew a cooking in the pot. It takes a mighty good camp cook to make anything that smells as good as that bunny rabbit. Don't tell me you made that stew, King!"

"Peg can't be beat for flavouring vittles," King praised warmly. "I don't know where he gets 'em, but he digs up some herbs and such here and there, and he provides most all the camp meat we need."

"I just don't have any manners," Tinsley told the boy. "Please, *cucinero*, could I have just a taste of that stew?"

"What's this shere *cucinero*?" Peg demanded.

"That's Spanish for cook," Tinsley explained quickly. "I'll never speak to you again if you go stingy on that rabbit stew."

"Puttin' 'er that away, yo're more than welcome," Pegasus muttered, and now there was a glint of pleasure in his dark eyes. He brought a clean plate from the wagon, ladled out a measure of stew, and handed it to the marshal. "You too?" Pegasus asked Carol.

"May I have some?" the girl asked eagerly.

"With shovel cake," Peg answered curtly, and went to the wagon for another plate.

Centaur King laid his gear aside and smacked his lips. Pegasus nodded and brought a heaping plate to the horse tamer, filled one for himself, and sat down with his back against a rear wheel of the wagon.

There was silence for a time as the four ate the flavoured stew. Pegasus Bronte started to dunk a slab of corn pone in the juice on his plate, and Centaur King coughed suggestively. Peg frowned and changed his mind, but Crag Tinsley laughed loudly. When Peg glared at the marshal, Tinsley winked and mopped his plate with a piece of corn bread.

"Pay no mind to Carol," Tinsley told Pegasus. "She's regular folks like you and me, and she don't put on any side."

"She ain't dunking," Peg declared stubbornly.

Carol Tinsley felt a flush of colour warming her cheeks. Here was a test of comradeship, and she knew that Centaur King was watching her. Taking a bit of corn bread, she dipped it in the rabbit gravy and popped it into her mouth. When she glanced at Peg Bronte, he was smiling at her in friendly fashion.

"I'll say she is," Peg agreed, and dipped his bread in the savoury juice.

"Miss Carol, you're a lady," Centaur King said soberly. "Are you really an artist?"

"I'll tell a man!" the marshal spoke for his sister. "She can paint a horse so's you can see the beast pawing up the ground!"

Peg Bronte listened and leaned forward. He started to speak, changed his mind, and turned to stare thoughtfully at the golden stallion in the pen.

"He's the purtiest thing in this world," the boy whispered.

"Can I paint him?" Carol pleaded earnestly. "I've loved El Caballo Oro for more than a year!"

"You couldn't love him near as much as me!" Peg answered hotly. "I'm sorry, Miss Carol," he excused himself. "You can paint him if you'll be careful and not get too close. Gold 'Un is a killer, and he will be until I get him gentled some."

"Weren't you afraid when he snapped at you?" Carol asked.

"Who, me?" Peg almost shouted, and then he lowered his head. "No'm," he continued quietly. "You ain't never afraid of anything you really loves with all yore heart!"

Carol Tinsley glanced at Centaur King, but she made no reply. Crag Tinsley asked for seconds on the rabbit stew, and Peg smiled to show his pleasure.

"Cowboy coffee coming right up," he announced, as he handed the marshal a second helping of stew. "Centaur always says not to put too much water in the coffee, but like as not it will be a mite too stout for Miss Carol."

"But I like strong coffee," Carol insisted. "With just a trace of sugar, and no milk to spoil the aroma."

"Dad-burn me if you don't talk man-size," Pegasus voiced his admiration. "I ain't never met a female gal like you in all my travels!"

"Thank you, Pegasus," Carol murmured gratefully. "And I promise not to go female on you, if you will promise to treat me like another man."

"She's a deal," Pegasus agreed with enthusiasm, and he extended his right hand. "Press the flesh, Miss Carol!"

Centaur King watched and listened, and smiled with content. Pegasus Bronte was a boy of high spirit, but he also had good breeding.

"You'll do to ride the river with, Peg," he told the boy, and Crag Tinsley smiled his understanding. In cattle country, no higher compliment could be given a man.

"That's what ever," the marshal added his say. "Might be you and Peg will take on a piece of land and locate in these parts, eh, King?"

Centaur King's face clouded slightly. "It's a fair land," he admitted. "As fair as many I've seen."

"You've travelled abroad?" Carol asked quickly.

"I'll say," Pegasus interrupted. "Centaur has tamed hosses for those sheiks in Arabia, and over in Spain. A man has to travel when he has . . . the gift!"

43

Centaur King quickly changed the subject. He asked Tinsley about the big ranches in the neighbourhood of Lanthrope, and Pegasus Bronte subsided with a flush on his thin face.

Carol studied the handsome face of the horse tamer as he talked of his work. Centaur King was perfectly poised, but there was no suggestion of arrogance about him. Only a quiet dignity and self-confidence which fitted the horse tamer like his tailored clothing.

"We start to work in the morning," King told the marshal. "Jim Stacey says we can use his corrals, and a man named Bailey was asking Stacey about my prices."

"You want to watch Sam Bailey," Tinsley warned gruffly. "He's a bit on the overbearing side."

"Centaur can handle him," Peg Bronte spoke up promptly. "There was a big hombre down Dallas way . . ."

"Not now, Peg," King interrupted quietly, but his deep voice was firm. "I like Jim Stacey," King changed the subject, and he smiled at the girl.

"Salt of the earth, and he knows hoss-flesh," Tinsley agreed, but he was watching his pretty sister.

"Do be careful of Sam Bailey," the girl warned King. "He is a big man, and he has a violent temper."

"Then he would never make a good hand with horses," King answered slowly. "Before a man can control horses, he has to learn a measure of self-control himself."

Pegasus Bronte gathered up the dishes and said he'd have to be getting at his chores. Twilight was closing in, and Carol suggested that it was time to be getting home.

"You will come to see us, you and Pegasus?" she asked, as she shook hands with King. "Now Crag will have to make excuses to Rose and Madeline because we ate supper here."

"She's a beautiful child," King answered with a smile. "Yes, we will come to see you all."

Peg Bronte was washing the dishes, and he called to the departing guests with his hands in the suds. When they were gone, Centaur King came to the tail-gate and cleared his throat. Peg glanced up and then continued scrubbing the crocks.

"You don't like Miss Carol?" King asked gently.

"Oh, she's all right, I reckon."

"You wouldn't be jealous because she loves El Caballo Oro?"

Peg shuffled his boots and shrugged his thin shoulders. "She's taken a shine to you," he growled just above his breath.

Centaur King appeared startled, and then he began to laugh. Peg glared at him and reached for the drying towel.

"I don't want no truck with women," he muttered. "And no more do you, was you to speak out and tell the truth!"

"Gently lad, gently," King said quietly. "We have so much to learn, you and me. I've spent most of my life learning about horses, and I know so little about women. Now Miss Carol seems different, and she thinks like a man."

"Over in California they raise plenty of fine horses," Peg changed the subject. "Mister Jim Stacey was telling me about them, and some day you and me will work our way over there."

"And up in Montana," King agreed with enthusiasm. "Look, Peg," he continued quietly. "I'd rather you didn't mention to folks about me travelling in foreign lands."

"I'm sorry, Centaur, but I got to thinking of those Spanish Barbs you tamed," the boy answered contritely. "Do you really think Gold 'Un is descended from those old hosses that Spaniard brought over here three-four hundred years ago?"

"I'm sure of it," King answered positively. "That horse loves you already, Peg."

"It's taken me six months to save up that gold," Peg answered soberly. "But he's worth every bit of it, and twice as much more."

King gathered up his ropes and gear and stowed them in the Conestoga wagon. Pegasus finished his dishes and took a turn around the neat camp to make everything secure for the night. Two bunks were built in the front end of the roomy wagon, and the two undressed and sought their blankets.

Pegasus Bronte was asleep almost instantly, but he woke with all his faculties alert when King placed a hand on the boy's forehead.

"Quiet, Peg, but we have a visitor," King whispered. "I don't know where she came from, but there's a golden mare near El Caballo's corral. Take this rope after you slip into your pants, and follow me!"

"A gal hoss," Peg muttered his disgust. "Let's grab up a chunk and run that stray off!"

"This one isn't a stray," King whispered. "Unless I'm wrong, it's a wild one wandered in from the hills to the south. Might be we could snare her."

The golden stallion blasted a shrill call as the two crept from the big wagon. Centaur King crouched in the shadows and pointed to the corral in the bright moonlight. Pegasus held his breath as he stared at a beautiful golden mare which stood with head high and tail curving.

"Oh!" Pegasus whispered. "She's so purty it hurts!"

"Unshod, and no mark of a rope or saddle," King murmured. "Unless we do something, Gold 'Un will break down that pen!"

"We can't shoot her," Peg almost whimpered.

"But if Gold 'Un gets away, he'll go back with the wild bunch!"

"Give me your catch-rope," King whispered. "I'll tie it to mine, and try a long cast. If I snare that beauty, we will take a sliding turn around the wagon axle. We might be able to choke her down without breaking her neck, and if my aim is true, you man the rope. Give just enough slack to keep her from getting up, but don't turn her loose unless you want me to get killed!"

Pegasus nodded and watched King place a drop of oil between his palms. The mare was close to the corral bars, and the stallion was screaming the mating call. The boy watched with mingled feelings of jealousy and love, and he could hear Centaur King laying out his coils just behind him.

"Take the end of the rope," King whispered, and he built a head-size loop in his lariat. "Pass it around the axle, but don't tie hard. Slip it if I'm lucky, but whatever, you stay here!"

Pegasus slipped under the wagon and took a turn around the axle with the tail end of the double catch-rope. Then he hunkered down to watch.

It was all of twenty yards to the corral where the wild mare stood in the moonlight. Pegasus watched Centaur King, and he saw the horse tamer getting ready to throw. The stallion blasted another shrill call, and King took advantage of the noise to whirl the loop once over his head.

The noose shot out like a hissing snake with the coils running smoothly. The wild mare heard the warning belatedly, and just as she made a desperate leap, the loop circled her head and snugged tight against her neck.

Pegasus Bronte leaned back instinctively as the mare tightened the slack. The wagon lurched a trifle as the mare hit the end of the rope and turned a hoolihan, tail over head. Then King was running forward, and Pegasus gave a little slack to keep the mare from choking.

"Easy gal, easy now," Peg heard King call softly, and the boy crouched under the wagon with his heart pumping against his ribs. He had learned much from Centaur King, but this was the first time he had seen King snare a wild one.

The stallion was whistling and striking the bars with his front hooves. Centaur King was going down the rope hand over hand, and the mare struggled to free herself. But now her breath was almost gone, and Peg watched as King stopped near the mare and began to mumble horse-talk.

Peg slacked off a little and then took a bight. The mare surged back, but she was too weak to get her front feet under her.

"Easy, lady," King soothed the frightened animal, and then his right hand touched her neck.

The mare trembled and began to snort. Centaur

49

King stroked the sweat-drenched neck as he continued to work his magic. With touch and voice, and that peculiar power which was given only to they who had the gift.

The mare quieted some, but the whites of her eyes showed as she watched this man-thing who dared to touch her. Centaur King extended his left hand slowly, and the mare bared her great teeth. King did not withdraw his hand; just kept talking in a mumbling whisper as his right hand stroked her neck.

"Gently, sweetheart," Peg heard King murmur, and the boy knew that the worst was over.

King pulled gently on the rope to indicate to Peg that he wanted more slack. Pegasus gave slowly, and King stretched erect. He spoke softly to the mare, patted her chest, and half turned his back.

The mare got her front feet under her, lurched up, and backed away. King spoke again without turning.

"Come here, lady. Come here, I say!"

The mare twitched her ears and took a tiny step forward. Another mincing step and she was smelling the shoulder of the man who had talked so soothingly when she was in distress. Now the rope was loose around her neck, and the golden stallion was also quiet.

"Come slowly and let down the bars," King whispered to the boy. "We will turn her in with

Gold 'Un, and tomorrow early we will move her to a stronger corral."

Pegasus crept slowly through the moonlight, talking softly as he advanced. The stallion whickered eagerly, and Peg let down the top bar. He stepped inside, ordered the stallion to a far corner, and let down the other bars.

Centaur King walked into the corral, and the mare followed meekly. King petted her, slowly removed the catch-rope, and stepped outside. Pegasus replaced the bars, followed King a little distance, and spoke reverently.

"She'd have killed me, Centaur. I was afraid she would lead Gold 'Un away, but now I love her!"

"So now you have two golden horses," King answered with a smile.

"You mean I can have her?" Peg asked incredulously.

"Those two go together like day and night, like sunshine and rain," Centaur King answered softly. "To please me, you'll call her . . . Lady?"

"Oh, yes," Pegasus promised eagerly, and then he stiffened. "Lady," he repeated in a whisper. "Now that other lady will want to paint her too!"

"Is it wrong to want to make beauty endure?" King asked quietly. "Sleep on it, lad. I'm going back to my bunk and pound my ear until daylight."

"I'll sleep on it," Pegasus muttered, "but I

don't like female women none to speak of. They always want something I want more than they do."

"What say?" King asked sharply.

"I said good-night," Pegasus grumbled, and then he crawled into his bunk without undressing.

# CHAPTER FOUR
## HORSE MAGIC

Centaur King was loosening up a pair of catch-ropes in a big corral behind the sales ring. It was the day after the auction, and buyers had taken the horse tamer at his word. They had brought him wild horses, many of which had been given up for hopeless, and a crowd was gathered to watch King work his magic.

Pegasus Bronte was gearing up the big black stallion just outside the corral. The golden stallion was penned in another corral, and he was watching the boy with ears pricked forward jealously. Peg smiled and called to his new purchase.

"I'll be with you-uns directly, Gold 'Un. I'm either going to top you off, or have it done!"

Another horse whinnied from a far pen, and Pegasus waved a small hand. Jim Stacey was admiring the golden mare, and he came over to talk to Peg Bronte.

"Beats me, it does," the auctioneer said slowly. "Yonder is a mare that like as not never felt a hand on her before. She comes right here to your camp, and King snares her with an uphill cast. All of sixty feet from the wagon to that corral, and

53

that's mighty long-range roping even for Texas."

"Her name is Lady," Peg told Stacey. "Centaur named her, and that suits me."

"Wait until Carol sees her," Stacey said, and he stared when Peg scowled at him. "You don't like Carol Tinsley?" he asked.

"I got me two golden hosses now," Peg answered grimly. "And Centaur is the best pard a man ever had!"

"Uh huh," Jim Stacey said quietly. "Well, I'll be getting over to see if I can help your pard."

Centaur King smiled at Stacey as he coiled his ropes. A tall lanky man strolled up and watched the horse tamer, and Stacey called the man by name.

"Howdy, Sam Bailey. When you going to ship those saddle-broncs to your ranch over in west Texas?"

"Presently," Bailey answered. "After I get some work done here, and mebbe make a little money on a wager or two."

"Now look, Bailey," Stacey warned the tall Texan. "I know your weakness for gambling, but don't get to crowding Centaur King."

"I never start to build something I can't put a roof over," Bailey answered arrogantly. "You forgetting those outlaws I bought for Rodeo work?"

"What about them?" Stacey demanded.

"Just listen in," Bailey answered, and turned

to watch Centaur King who was getting ready to mount the black stallion.

"Howdy, Bailey," King said courteously.

"Yeah," Bailey grunted. "You think you can gentle that big bay gelding?" he drawled, and his puckered eyes held a hint of derision.

King glanced at Bailey and his face hardened.

"I think so," he answered quietly. "If I don't, you save the fee of twenty-five dollars I asked."

"I'll make you a sportin' proposition," Bailey offered. "A hundred dollars on the side that you can't stay with him for a full minute!"

"Peg!" King called softly. "Come over here and hold Major Domo."

Peg Bronte nodded and came to hold the black stallion. He looked at King and then at Bailey, and he showed no surprise when King spoke again.

"Take a hundred dollars from Mr. Bailey," King told the boy. "Put a hundred of our money with it, and give it to Jim Stacey to hold. I've just made a trifling bet with Bailey that I can ride that bay gelding a full minute."

"You mean just to set on that knothead a minute," the boy corrected. "If Mr. Bailey is feeling blooded this morning, I'd like a hundred of the same!"

Pegasus pulled a canvas sack from inside his shirt and counted out gold pieces. He raised his brown eyes questioningly as he glanced at Bailey.

Bailey dug deep and counted out two hundred in gold as other cattlemen gathered around. Peg Bronte handed the money to Stacey and picked up one of the catch-ropes.

"Clear the corral," he said sharply. "It's time for me and Centaur to start our chores!"

"Them's day orders, and yo're the ramrod," a grizzled old cowman chuckled, as he led the way to the bars and climbed to the top rail.

Centaur King mounted the black stallion and built a head-sized loop in his grass lariat. Two stout posts had been set in the ground in the middle of the corral, about fifteen feet apart. King rode to a gate and Pegasus slid the bar. The boy climbed the fence and flicked his rope at a vicious bay gelding which spilled into the big corral, bawling with rage.

Centaur King studied the horse, and he knew something of its history. The bay had eaten the roots of loco weed, and the powerful narcotic had destroyed its reason. King also knew that the condition was aggravated after a fast run when the blood got hot, but this was a secret he kept to himself.

As the bay rushed past King, the horse tamer shot his loop and snared the tossing head. He took his dallies around the saddle-horn as Major Domo sat back to take up the slack. The bay hit the end of the rope and busted itself, turning over backward in the thick dust.

King touched Major Domo with a heel and rode up to the front snubbing post. Stepping lightly down from the saddle, King passed his rope around the post and snubbed the bay's head tight and low as the outlaw scrambled to its feet. After finishing his ties, King nodded slightly at his helper.

Pegasus Bronte darted behind the struggling horse and dabbed his loop on the ground at the kicking heels. He caught the left leg, tightened his twine, and stepped back to take a bight around the rear post. Little by little he took up the slack until the bay's left hind leg was stretched out. Then the boy tied fast and hunkered down on his heels to watch.

"Nice roping, men," Dapper Jim Stacey praised heartily. "And that bay never had a chance to get up a sweat!"

Centaur King glanced at Peg Bronte and winked. He was teaching the boy some of his secrets, and Peg nodded soberly. King walked over and hunkered down beside his helper.

"We'll have to keep that bay penned up for a month," he said, just loud enough for Pegasus to hear. "Feed him a handful of linseed meal with his grain. It's a mild physic, and it will take that long to work the loco weed out of his system. When you ride him, don't let him run and get hot. Now get the pack-saddle ready!"

Here was another trade secret between the

master and his pupil. Pegasus Bronte had vowed that he would never make common knowledge of his learning, and he sniffed when King took the tiny vial from his pocket and poured a drip of the colourless liquid on his left palm. Peg fetched a heavy pack-saddle close to the stretched-out bay which had now stopped fighting.

"I use a drop of this rare and secret oil," King told the boy. "I can't tell you what it is, but even a wolf won't bite you if your hands are protected with just one drop, providing the critter gets the scent first. For that reason, always reach out slow when you touch a vicious hoss."

"You could do it without that magic oil," Pegasus declared positively. "I've seen you do it several times when you forgot about the oil. You want I should talk to that ornery no-account bay?"

"You save your wind to talk to Golden," King answered with a little smile, and picked up the pack-saddle.

"All this mumbo jumbo," Sam Bailey complained to Jim Stacey. "Is he gonna fit a ride on that locoed bronc, or is he just gonna sit there and whisper in its off ear?"

"Yeah," Stacey said lazily.

"What you mean, yeah?" Bailey demanded truculently.

"Yeah, he's going to fit a ride on that bay," Stacey answered without looking at Bailey. "You better watch, and you might learn a thing or two."

The bay twitched when the saddle touched its back. Centaur King began to talk in a weird jumble as his hands soothed the trembling horse. Peg Bronte went to the other side and fastened the cinchas. Then he picked up a hundred-pound sack of oats with an ease that made the watchers stare.

The boy lifted the sack high and laid it on the pack-saddle. King passed him the tie-ropes, and the sack was lashed securely in place. Sam Bailey tipped a bottle, drank generously, and voiced his disgust.

"I thought you was going to top off that boy!" he shouted at King.

Centaur King made no answer, and he didn't even glance at Bailey. He sat down on his heels and talked in low tones to Pegasus Bronte while the long minutes ticked away. After fifteen minutes, Sam Bailey could no longer contain himself.

"Bring me wild ones, he says! Then he breaks 'em out for pack-hosses!"

"Quiet, Bailey," Stacey warned, but the cattle-man took another pull at his bottle as he glared at King. When the horse tamer paid no attention, Bailey crawled between the bars, walked up behind King, and nudged him with a rusty boot. A spot of vivid colour appeared on the horse tamer's high cheek-bones, but he controlled his sudden anger. He even smiled at Peg Bronte.

Sam Bailey scowled then and kicked the horse tamer gently with his boot. Centaur King uncoiled like a steel spring and whirled as he arose. His two hands shot out and fastened on Sam Bailey's biceps, picked the big man up with ridiculous ease, and then King whirled in a half circle.

Bailey's feet left the ground as his bulky body began to swing. Centaur King loosened his grip, and Bailey sailed over the corral fence to land with a thud on the outside.

"Never enter a ring when I am at work," Centaur King said softly, but his deep, resolute voice vibrated with a terrible rage.

Pegasus Bronte narrowed his brown eyes and nodded his tousled head in understanding. He had a kinship of spirit with this master of wild horses, and some day he too would attain to the same high level. After a long moment of silence, King spoke softly to the boy.

"Get the short rope ready, Peg. Tie it firmly to the bay's tail!"

Silent cattlemen watched with keen interest; men who had believed that they knew all the tricks of breaking the bad one. Pegasus caught up a short soft rope, approached the bay, and passed his thin strong hands over the muscular flanks. Mumbling softly under his breath, he worked down and backward until he had reached the bay's thick tail.

A slip-noose went over the tail and was braided in with the long strands of horse-hair. Centaur King came around and took the end of the rope which he passed under the bay's neck. His left hand touched the horse and stroked gently, and then King made his tie.

Now the bay was tied head-to-tail with its tail between his hind legs. The bay's head was pulled down and back, and Peg Bronte threw off the rope which held the left hind leg out-stretched. Centaur King threw off the ties which held the bay's head snubbed low to the post, after which he led the horse away from the stout logs.

Sam Bailey was leaning against the bars with a scowl on his beefy face. A heavy six-shooter rode in the open holster on his right leg, ready to his hand. If King noticed either the weapon or the threat, he gave no sign.

King handed the end of the lass-rope to Pegasus and the boy started to walk the bay around the corral, carrying the pack-saddle. Centaur King walked slowly to Major Domo and removed his plain hand-made saddle. He had fashioned the hull with his own hands, but he inspected the gear thoroughly. If a latigo or sling broke during a rough ride, a man just might come up with broken bones.

Slipping the light head-stall over the black stallion's head, King fitted the loop in the short thong over the stallion's right front foot. Major Domo would stand as though he were tied to a tree, and he nuzzled King affectionately as the horse tamer turned to study the boy. Then King spoke to Peg Bronte.

"Bring the bay here," King called, and the boy obeyed instantly.

That was just one more of the things Peg Bronte had learned. King always thought each move out in advance, and in any team, he had explained to Peg, every man had to know his job and do it without hesitation.

Centaur King began to talk softly as he worked. His left hand pulled the ropes holding the sack of grain which he lifted to the ground with one hand. Then he pulled the latigo and removed the heavy pack-saddle. Again his hands soothed the horse a time or two while the silent watchers strained their ears in an effort to understand what King was saying to the outlaw horse.

King held his left hand out and allowed the bay to sniff gingerly. Then he laid his saddle-blanket on the broad back, keeping up his low-voiced mumbling. The handmade saddle was raised and placed gently on the bay, and King caught the latigo and tightened the cinchas.

"Mebbe this Fancy Dan is really going to step aboard," Sam Bailey muttered, but Jim Stacey only nodded his head. The dapper auctioneer was too absorbed in watching the work of a master, and Bailey was just one more cattleman among many.

"Ready, Pegasus?" King asked the boy.

"Ready, Centaur," Peg Bronte answered with the respect of equality.

Peg stepped around to the far side and placed his hand on the vicious bay's flank. Centaur King turned the left stirrup, caught the saddle-horn with his right hand, and swung up as lightly as a feather. The test was about to begin.

The bay twitched and flattened its ears. Peg Bronte was loosening the horse hair from the loop which held the tail. A slow step and he pulled the knot which held the bay's head down.

Centaur King was in the saddle, with only the coils of his lass-rope in his left hand. The loop was about the outlaw's neck, but there was no trapping on its head.

The bay raised its head and shook gently. Then it took a forward step as King nudged lightly with a heel. The bay lowered its head suddenly and started bucking, and Centaur King shook the loop loose and threw the bay's head away. That is, he was riding by balance and skill alone, and the outlaw was free to make its own fight.

"Kill the son," Stacey heard Sam Bailey mutter. "He's all show and no metal, and I hope the bay tromps him to rags!"

"For how much?" Stacey asked quietly, and

he turned to face Bailey with a flat wallet in his hand.

Bailey shrugged and refused the challenge. His eyes were blood-shot, and his right hand was still close to the gun-handles on his thick leg.

"I hope Mister King knows what he is doing," a frightened voice whispered, and Stacey turned to smile reassuringly at Carol Tinsley who had just arrived to watch the ride.

"Don't you worry none about Centaur King," the auctioneer told the pretty girl. "There he comes apart!"

Swallowing its head between hairy fetlocks, the bay humped its back like a maddened cat. Then it started a series of sun-fishing bucks with all four feet off the ground in a move the bronc-riders called: "sunning its belly."

Centaur King loosened his supple back and rode out the storm with a little smile of enjoyment curling his lips.

"All right, boy," he said softly, speaking intelligibly for the first time, and his free right hand slapped the bay on the neck.

The horse stopped bucking instantly, and King relaxed. He had matched wits and skill with everything the bay had to offer, and the ride was apparently over.

Then a booming explosion shattered the stillness as Sam Bailey drew his gun and fired into the ground under the now docile bay.

The horse lowered its ears and listened, and Centaur King gently stroked the lowered neck. Then King nudged with his left heel, touched the bay with his right hand, and rode along the fence at a walk.

Just opposite Sam Bailey, the horse tamer left the saddle in a swift lunge with his arms spread wide. Swiftly as a hunting lance, the muscled frame of Centaur King lunged at Sam Bailey and knocked the cattleman to the ground. The gun spilled from Bailey's fingers as the two men hit the ground, but Centaur King followed through and rolled up to his feet.

Without saying a word to Bailey, King crawled back through the bars, walked slowly up to the bay which was standing quiet, and removed his saddle. Peg Bronte caught King's eye and winked slowly.

Marshal Crag Tinsley was now standing beside his sister, watching Sam Bailey with a grim smile on his rugged features. Bailey struggled to his feet, dusted off his clothes, but made no attempt to recover his gun from the dust.

Carrying his gear over his left arm, Centaur King walked over, nodded at Tinsley, tipped his Stetson to Carol, and spoke quietly to Jim Stacey.

"I'll take my winnings now, Jim," he said in his slow drawl. "Peg and I will split the take, and then we will be getting along with our chores. Sam Bailey will have a right good horse if he treats that bay properly, and if he don't the horse will like as not kill him."

"And none would miss him," Crag Tinsley spoke gruffly. "I was watching him with that belt gun, and it's a good thing he didn't raise his sights!"

Sam Bailey listened and turned his broad back. He was very careful as he picked up his six-shooter which he snugged slowly down into his holster. Then the cattleman walked away with his shoulders hunched forward, and Peg Bronte led the bay to a small corral with a loose rope. He and Centaur King had to earn their living, and there were other horses to break.

66

# CHAPTER FIVE
## THE TEST

Pegasus Bronte glanced at the sun, a coppery disc hovering just above the western horizon. Centaur King was working with a dappled Percheron whose owner said the big draft animal weighed a ton. King had gentled five horses since riding the bay, using a different method with each, according to the faults and dispositions of the various animals.

The Percheron was called "Big Mac," and had suddenly acquired the vicious habit of biting. It was eight years old and had been broken to harness to work in the grain fields. Peg Bronte knew that King was almost finished with the big Percheron, but he was watching every movement carefully, to learn the secrets of the laying-on-of-hands.

Peg widened his eyes when Centaur King walked over to a horse trough and washed his hands thoroughly. Now there would be no magic oil to soothe the big beast tied to one of the snubbing posts. Pegasus studied King's thin, sensitive face with an expression of reverence in his glowing dark eyes.

The boy was sensitive himself, but he tried to

cover up what he considered a weakness with an exaggerated exterior of toughness. Centaur King was always quiet and self-contained, except on those rare occasions when his temper would spill over, as in the case of Sam Bailey and the six-shooter.

Centaur possessed a soothing magnetic touch to which animals responded instinctively. His voice was gently persuasive, and there were those who said he was really half-man and half-horse, as his first name implied. That he possessed "the gift" was readily admitted, which fact and legend declared came only once in a century.

King dried his hands and walked slowly back to the Percheron. The big horse raised its huge head with lips curling back over great yellowed teeth. Centaur King extended his left hand slowly for the horse to sniff, talking meanwhile just above his breath.

Big Mac slowly stretched his neck and sniffed the extended hand with flaring nostrils. The curling lips stopped snarling as the horse nuzzled the horse tamer's hand. Centaur King reached up slowly and took the right ear in his left hand. The Percheron obediently lowered its head, and King whispered for a long moment in the ear of the big horse.

The Percheron blinked wisely and slowly nodded. How much was hocus pocus and how much skill was difficult for the watchers to judge.

Jim Stacey knew that King was a good showman, but the dapper auctioneer also believed firmly in the horse tamer's powers.

The crowd of cattlemen and horse traders watched curiously as King stepped back and walked slowly away with the Percheron following like a great docile dog. Into a small corral at the heels of the master, and Pegasus Bronte closed the swinging gates without sound.

"He won't bite any more," Centaur King told the grain farmer. "After this, don't let anyone tease Big Mac. He's too big for such treatment, and he could break a bone in a man's arm with one crunch."

"How'd you know?" the surprised rancher gasped. "Mac like to have killed a hand I had working, who had a habit of eating apples in front of the horse, offering him a bite, and then taking it himself!"

"And then slapping at Big Mac," King added. "My fee is ten dollars, and you can take Big Mac home with you now."

Crag Tinsley touched King on the arm and made a gesture with his head. Little Madeline was talking to Pegasus Bronte with adoration in her rounded blue eyes.

"Look at those two," the marshal chuckled. "It's love at first sight with Madeline, and Peg don't know what to do."

Centaur King made a motion for Tinsley to stay

back, and both men sat down on their heels. Peg Bronte was looking at the little three-year-old, and trying to act as though he didn't see her.

"I like you, Peg," the child said gravely.

"Gwan," Peg growled. "How'd you know my name, Little Bit?"

"'At's what my Daddy says," Madeline answered with a smile. "Daddy says that all good things come in small packages."

"Yeah, and so does pizen," Pegasus answered coldly. "You better run along now, and let a man do the work he gets paid for doing."

"Yes, I know," Madeline agreed humbly. "You and Mister King are horse tamers, and I like Mister King a heap."

"Aw, like who don't," Peg answered, without looking at the child.

"Are you really a horse tamer?" Madeline asked in an awed whisper.

"Well, you stick around and watch me work," Peg growled. "Mind you stay back out of the way, and don't go walking under horses like you did yesterday."

"Mister King didn't fuss with me," Madeline said with a little pout.

"He should have warped you a couple with the back of his hand," Peg said sternly. "Tell you what," he added, and his face softened some. "You sit up there on that block and promise not to move until I tell you. I've got to fit a ride on a killer, and I don't want you gettin' in my way."

"Cross my heart and hope to die if I move from the block," Madeline promised, and gravely crossed herself on the right side. Peg Bronte sniffed, but he picked up the little girl and carried her to Stacey's auction block. Madeline circled his neck with her plump little arms, and Peg scowled with simulated fierceness.

"Now you stay put there, Little Bit," he admonished, as he placed her on the shelf. "I got more important things on my mind than playin' nursemaid to a little ole gal-chip."

"Yes, Peg," Madeline replied meekly. "You won't forget to come back and get me, will you, Peg?"

"*Hasta la vista*," Peg growled.

"What did you say?"

"Said I'd be seeing you pretty soon," Peg barked, and turning his back, he walked away.

Crag Tinsley touched Centaur King on the arm and spoke quietly, but with a worried undertone in his deep voice.

"The little feller," he whispered. "Is he sure enough going to work that golden stud over?"

"Sure enough," King answered with a slow smile. "Peg and I talked it all over, and I'm sure that he can handle the stallion. I am going to ask everyone to remain silent while Pegasus tries out some secrets he has learned. That lad is a natural with horses."

71

"Quiet, please," Dapper Jim Stacey called to the crowd which thronged against the rails of the show ring. "Peg Bronte is going to work on his own hoss, and we might all learn something. Don't shoot off that gun of yours again, Sam Bailey!"

Bailey scowled and felt of his bruised muscles where the steely fingers of Centaur King had bitten deep. Bailey weighed two hundred pounds, fifty more than the horse tamer who had thrown him across the corral fence with ridiculous ease. Like the big Percheron, Sam Bailey had been broken of a bad habit, and every man around the sales ring knew it.

Carol Tinsley came close to Centaur King who turned to the girl with a contagious smile. "I'm afraid Mr. King," Carol whispered. "Pegasus looks so slight, and El Caballo Oro is so big and strong."

"Did you see Peg's new love?" King asked.

"You mean the golden mare?"

"Yes, I mean Lady," King answered. "She was a wild one until midnight, but when I got up this morning, Peg was whispering in her ear. What's more, Lady liked it."

"May I stand here with you?" Carol asked.

"Please do," King answered heartily. "I'm proud of Peg Bronte, and I want you to see why."

Pegasus Bronte was arranging his gear along the west fence of the big corral. The great golden

72

stallion was in a small holding pen, watching the boy with his proud head over the top rail. Centaur King held his place outside the ring, between Carol Tinsley and the marshal. Jim Stacey was watching every move critically, and he turned to King.

"You're not going to help him, Centaur?" Stacey whispered anxiously.

"Pegasus needs no help," King answered confidently. "He is learning fast, and I believe that he has the gift!"

Quiet fell across the show ring as the golden sun slipped down beyond the distant horizon. Pegasus Bronte laid out two catch-ropes neatly coiled, a short tie-rope, and a stock saddle. He also had the gift of showmanship, and the ability to concentrate.

The golden stallion watched as the boy went to the horse trough and washed his hands in the clear cold water. Pegasus dried his hands on a rug he had tied to a rail. He took a small vial from one of the pockets of his white riding breeches, pulled the cork with his teeth, poured a drop of the colourless liquid in the palm of one hand, and returned the vial to his pocket. Then he turned to study the great golden horse as he carefully kneaded his palms together.

"That magic oil must be something like catnip," Stacey whispered to Crag Tinsley.

"Nuh uh," the marshal whispered back. "It had

no smell to it that I could tell, and like as not it's just to soften the hands. Hosses are sensitive that away, you know."

Centaur King made no explanation. He was watching his pupil with a slow little smile of affection curling the corners of his generous mouth. None but Centaur King knew that Pegasus had spent hours with the big horse before daybreak, brushing the sleek coat, and talking a language which only horses seem to understand.

Peg Bronte walked slowly to the gate of the holding pen and swung it open. The big stallion made a rush and leaped into the sales ring with head down and ears laid back, and his great teeth snapping viciously.

Pegasus picked up a small whip and closed the gate. He walked to the centre of the ring, flicked his whip at the stallion, and followed the animal when it began to circle the ring. His lips did not move for ten minutes as he made the stallion gallop around the corral, barely touching the satiny flank to keep the big horse in constant motion.

The stallion was thoroughly warmed up now, and getting restive. Pegasus Bronte turned his back with the little whip tucked under his left arm. Then he spoke very softly.

"Come here, Gold 'Un. Come here, I say!"

The big stallion stopped and pricked up its ears. Then it took one dainty step forward and hesitated. Bronte repeated his gentle command.

"Come here to me, Gold 'Un!"

The golden stallion minced up behind the boy and nuzzled Peg's left shoulder gently. Pegasus turned and reached out a hand slowly. The stallion sniffed a time or two and whickered softly.

The boy moved with deliberate slowness. He reached inside his jacket and brought out the light head-stall with the looped thong attached. When he shaped it in his hands, the stallion lowered his head. The boy slipped the head-stall on gently and, taking the looped thong, he led the stallion to the front snubbing post.

Centaur King knew all the emotions which were surging through the heart and mind of his young pupil. He was sure that Pegasus had no fear, but only a great love for the golden horse he had bought with his savings. King told himself that perhaps the gift had been given to two men in the same century as he watched with a quiet smile of perfect confidence.

King stopped breathing for a moment when Carol Tinsley leaned against him the better to watch the boy. Her firm rounded shoulder was cool against the hard muscles of his arm, and Centaur King stood motionless. Horses had been his life, and he knew so very little about women.

"Please be careful, Peg," King heard the girl murmur, and it was like a little prayer he shared with her.

Pegasus Bronte tied the light thong to the snubbing post and walked over to the rail where he had laid his saddle and blanket. The palomino stallion stood perfectly still, following every movement of the boy with his great brown eyes. The horse could have broken the thong with one twitch of his head, but something stronger than ropes was holding him obedient.

Peg came slowly across the ring, carrying his saddle. He stopped at the left side, and his right hand stroked the stallion's sleek neck. He laid his blanket on the satiny back, and carefully lifted his saddle into place.

The big horse quivered, and Pegasus began to talk in what Jim Stacey said must be the gift of tongues. No man could understand the weird mutterings, but the restive horse became instantly quiet. The boy reached under the high belly and caught the cinch, drawing his latigo through the ring, while his voice soothed the golden stallion until the saddle was cinched in place.

Would his magic hold out while Pegasus Bronte made the little jump necessary to reach the high stirrup? Would the great golden stud let this half-grown boy get firmly seated before he broke in two and came apart?

Centaur King asked himself these questions and many more. He seemed surprised when something moved under his left hand, and glancing down, he saw his hand gripping Carol's right arm.

"I'm sorry," he murmured contritely. "Did I hurt you, Carol?"

"Oh, no, and please do call me Carol," the girl whispered happily. "You do love Pegasus, don't you, Centaur King?"

"As much as one man can love another," King answered soberly. "Will you look at him now!"

Pegasus Bronte took the great muzzle in his two hands and laid his cheek against the stallion's jowl. His low voice crooned softly for a moment, then he reached for the saddle-horn with his right hand. One little leap and a pull, and he was on the hurricane deck and in the glory seat.

He shot his jockey boots deep into the oxbows, and it seemed then that he became a living part of the great golden stallion. With the light looped thong in his left hand, he was ready for the big test which would bring the answer as to whether or not he possessed the gift!

El Caballo Oro lowered his head and leaped high into the air. His heels scraped sky as he humped his back like a cat on the fight, but the boy on his back rode out the storm with a confident smile on his thin, tanned face. Then he deliberately tossed the thonged loop over the stallion's tossing head.

"He threw his head away!" Jim Stacey gasped. "Now it's him and the stud, with no holds barred!"

The stallion jumped sideward with all four feet

in the air. He bucked high and buckled a knee on the drop, reared high with front hoofs pawing, and then rushed off for the far fence. When it seemed that he was about to crash, the big stallion slid to a stop with all four feet bunched. Then he stopped and slowly raised his magnificent head.

Centaur King heard a little moan close to his ear. He had forgotten everything except Pegasus and the golden killer. Now he found Carol Tinsley close to him, and his own strong right arm about her waist, holding her close. King gasped and glanced at the marshal and Jim Stacey, but the two men were watching the duel in the ring. King gradually loosened his arm, and he tried not to hear the little sigh of disappointment which gusted from Carol's lips.

Pegasus Bronte loosed his boots and kicked the stirrups free. He reached down and caught the dangling loop with his left hand, and laid it against the golden neck on the left side. The stallion turned to the right and walked about the ring with mincing fiddle-footing steps of restrained power.

"Whoa, boy," Peg murmured.

The golden stallion stopped instantly. Peg slid down the left side and started walking away. The stallion followed him with head just over Peg's shoulder, and when they reached the snubbing posts, the boy stripped his gear and laid his saddle on the ground with the skirts turned up to catch the air.

Centaur King watched with a queer little feeling of jealousy and pride. He had been twelve years old when he had discovered that he had a way with vicious horses. He had developed his skill during the long lonely eighteen years which had followed, and now he was sharing that gift with another orphan.

Pegasus Bronte turned to face the golden stallion. His arms went up and around the curving neck, and the stallion lifted his new master from his feet and high into the air. Then he gently lowered the boy until Peg's boots touched the ground again, and whickered softly as Peg poured out his love in simple Deep South talk.

"I loves you, Gold 'Un," the boy half-sobbed. "Loves you so dad-burned much I can feel it way down inside. Don't ever aim to abuse or mis-use you in any way a-tall. Gosh, Gold 'Un, let's get gone out of here away from all these shere folks."

# CHAPTER SIX
## GOOD MANNERS

Little Madeline Tinsley watched Peg Bronte lead the golden stallion to a high-boarded pen. Her blue eyes were round with wonder and worship. Her pretty face changed when Pegasus bolted the pen gate and hurried from the show ring. She seemed to shrink as her tiny shoulders drooped, and tears formed in her winking eyes.

"Peggie," she cried softly. "Don't forget me, Peggie!"

Crag Tinsley heard the heart-broken plaint, and he hurried to his daughter's side. He tried to gather her up in his arms, but Madeline pushed him away.

"I promised," she wailed. "I even crossed my heart!"

Centaur King heard the cry and hurried to the platform. Madeline reached out her arms, but she refused to leave. King did not smile as he remembered what he had heard Pegasus Bronte say to the child.

"I won't ever leave here," Madeline cried. "I promised Peggie I'd stay until he came to get me."

"I know, sweetheart," King soothed the little

girl. "You just brighten up now, and I'm sure that Peg will be right back as soon as he puts his gear away!"

Centaur King hurried across the ring, and he found Peg Bronte at the Conestoga wagon. The boy looked up with a smile which fled from his expressive face when he saw King observing him grimly.

"I've never known you to break a promise, Pegasus," King said slowly. "You'd keep your spoken word if it killed you."

"I'll tell a man," Peg answered quickly.

"Have you forgotten?" King asked quietly.

"Oh, you mean Lady," the boy said. "I'm just about to feed her now."

"This concerns another lady," King answered gravely. "A lady you made promise you something."

"Naw I never," Peg denied indignantly. "I don't want no truck with ladies!"

"About so high," King continued, making a measurement of height with one hand. "Her first name is Madeline."

"Oh gee," Peg burst out. "I went off and left her a-sittin' on the platform. I forgot her, Centaur."

"So you'll do the needful?" King asked.

Peg Bronte dug a hole in the dust with the toe of one boot. Finally he nodded sullenly, hitched up his pants, and tugged his hat low over his dark eyes. Then he drew a deep breath and squared his shoulders.

"Yeah," he agreed reluctantly. "But I don't see why she didn't go on home with her folks."

He left the wagon and made his way slowly to the sales ring. Peg scowled when he saw Jim Stacey and the marshal at the platform. His lips tightened when he saw Carol Tinsley smiling at him, and he walked directly to the little girl and glared at her.

"You can get down now," he said ungraciously. "And thanks a lot for keeping yore promise!"

"Lift me down, Peggie," the little girl demanded, and held out her chubby arms.

"Yore Dad will lift you down," Peg growled.

"I want you to lift me down, Peggie!"

"Quit callin' me Peggie!" the boy burst out angrily.

"Ooh," Madeline wailed. "You're mad with me when I kept my promise!"

"Don't start to crying," Peg said quickly. "I'll lift you down, and then you can go home!"

He took the little girl in his arms, and Madeline tightened her arms around his neck. She refused to be put down, and Peg Bronte stood awkwardly with the little girl in his arms.

"I love you, Peggie," she murmured in his ear.

"Are you gonna quit callin' me Peggie?"

"You don't love me," Madeline wailed, and

she began to cry with her face buried against his tanned cheek.

Crag Tinsley turned away with a queer expression in his grey eyes. Carol Tinsley swallowed as she winked away a tear, and Jim Stacey turned his back. Peg Bronte stared at the three, and then he turned away with the child in his arms. His lower lips quivered, and then his arms tightened.

"Don't you cry no more, Sugar-foots," he whispered gently. "Old Peg was just tormentin' you, and he didn't mean a thing he said. Honest Injun, Sugar. Cross my heart and hope to die!"

Madeline stopped sobbing and turned her head slightly to listen. Then she raised her tear-stained face, and kissed him full on the lips.

"Hold me tight, Peggie," she pleaded. "I stayed right here like you told me."

"Peg," the boy said stubbornly. "Leave me hear you say just plain Peg!"

"Just plain Peg," Madeline repeated, and tightened her arms.

"Peg," the boy insisted. "You cussed little knot-head!"

"You don't love me," Madeline wailed, and Peg Bronte tightened his arms hastily.

"Shore I do, Sugar Foots," he said desperately.

"What's Sugar Foots?"

" 'At there's something you call a gal when she's real purty like you," Peg explained. "But not when you're crying all over the place," he added caustically.

"I won't cry any more, Peggie . . . Peg," the little girl promised, and reaching up, she kissed him again.

"Aw quit it, Little Bit," Peg pleaded. "All them grown folks is watching you and making fun of me. I'll see you to-morrow, huh, Sugar Foots?"

"Promise," Madeline insisted. "Cross your heart and hope to die?"

"Oh, I reckon," Peg answered reluctantly. "I'll be seeing you around."

"Cross your heart?"

"Cross my heart and spit," Peg answered sullenly. "*Adios*."

"Kiss me," Madeline demanded imperiously.

"Aw . . ."

"You don't love me," the little girl wailed.

Peg hastily bent his head and kissed Madeline on the cheek. She smiled at him and tightened her arms around his neck and a sudden change came over the boy. His lips kissed her ear, and he smiled when Madeline turned to look at him.

"I'll be your big brother," Peg said softly. "I never had a little sister, and I do love you, Sugar Foots."

Crag Tinsley gulped and blinked his eyes. Peg Bronte walked up to the marshal and spoke gravely.

"Mister Tinsley, do you mind, Suh, if I sotter be

a big brother to Sugar Foots?" he asked earnestly.

"Bless you, son," the marshal said gruffly. "I'll be as happy as all out doors about it. Press the flesh, feller!"

The two shook hands heartily, and Jim Stacey blew his nose. Peg Bronte handed Madeline to her father and ran back to the big wagon. He went straight to Centaur King and spoke gravely.

"I love that little rascal, Centaur," he stated manfully. "I'm going to be her big brother!"

"Rather sudden, wasn't it?" King asked with a little smile of understanding.

That was one of the things Peg Bronte liked about Centaur King. Centaur didn't laugh *at* a feller; he laughed with him.

"Hit me like a bolt of heat lightnin'," Peg admitted honestly. "I dunno, Centaur. All I wanted was to get away from that little gal, and then she started in to blubbering. Made me feel like I had kicked a li'l ole cuddly dog."

"Yes, I know," King answered softly. "Then she hugged up close to you, and you knew how little and helpless like she was, and it somehow made you feel about twice as big. You wanted to kinda look after her and see that she didn't get bumped around and hurt."

"Say! How'd you know that?" the boy whispered.

"I always wanted a little sister," King answered wistfully. "Someone to spoil, and to sotter . . .

you know what I mean . . . mebbe love a little?"

"Yeah," Peg murmured. "They kinda sneak into a feller's tough ole heart. Course they bother a man," he added thoughtfully. "They're always gonna see you tomorrow, and they want a lot of waiting on."

"Uh huh," King agreed with a nod. "But it's a funny thing that away, pard. When you get to loving 'em, it don't seem like a bother any more."

"Well, I got to feed Lady and gentle her up some," Peg changed the subject, but King noticed an expression of gentleness he had never noticed before in Peg Bronte.

King watched while Peg forked blue-stem to the mare, talking all the while to the spooky animal. When Peg measured out some rolled barley and shook the can suggestively, the golden mare pricked up her ears. Then she inched forward, stretching her neck to smell the can.

"Closer," Peg said softly. "Come up just a little bit closer, Lady."

But the mare drew back and sulked in a corner. Centaur King watched to see what the boy would do. Peg Bronte climbed through the bars, and the mare shied away. The boy seemed to ignore her as he poured the grain in the bin, and then he left the pen without another word to the wondering mare.

"That's the system," King praised quietly. "Take it easy and wait for them to come to you.

Lady will be nuzzling your shoulder within a week."

"I'll start supper," Peg said, and Centaur King busied himself with the camp chores. After eating, he helped Peg with the dishes, and the boy spoke carelessly.

"Reckon it would be all right if I bought a doll I saw in town, and carried it up to Sugar Foots?" he asked.

Centaur King glanced quickly at the boy who kept his eyes on a skillet he was washing.

"Here now," King said gruffly. "Isn't Miss Carol too big to play with a doll?"

"Nobody said anything about that artist," Peg answered crossly. "Madeline ain't no more than a baby, and the marshal said I could be her big brother."

"I beg your pardon, Pegasus," King apologized with a smile. "I think it would be just fine, and if you don't mind, I'll walk up with you."

"It's that Miss Carol," Peg burst out, and then he stopped scowling. "I reckon mebbe she wants a big brother too," he added soberly. "Say! Wait up a spell," he corrected himself. "She has a brother; the marshal!"

"Yeah, that's right," King agreed. "You run along, and I'll stay here and talk some to Lady."

Peg sighed and spoke reluctantly. "We always go places together, pard. I'd admire for to have your company."

"You don't want me to talk to Lady?" King asked lazily.

The boy shrugged uncomfortably. "I sotter wanted to put the spell on her my ownself," he admitted. "You mind very much, Centaur?"

"Not at all," King answered quickly. "I know just how you feel, feller."

"I won't go up to see Madeline unless you come along," the boy spoke positively. "I was ornery to her, Centaur."

"I'll shave and clean up a bit," King said, and climbed into the wagon.

Peg Bronte grunted and muttered that there was no call to slick all up just to see a little ole gal-chip who would have to go to bed by eight o'clock at the latest, but if King heard him, he gave no sign. He had changed to a fresh whipcord suit when he joined the boy, and Peg sniffed his disapproval.

Down in town, Centaur King bought a box of candy while Peg bought the doll he had seen.

"Let's eat some of it now," Peg suggested. "I ain't had a bite of pokey for quite a spell."

"Do you mind if we wait?" King asked evasively. "We don't want to forget all our manners, Pegasus. Ladies come first, you know."

"Then you did buy it for her," Peg accused bluntly. "That's for why you got all slicked up in your town clothes!"

"Yes," King said very softly. "You want to make something out of it?"

"You take the doll up to Sugar Foots," Peg almost whispered. "I wish we were packing up and rolling for California to-morrow!"

Centaur King stopped and stared at the sullen boy. Then he smiled and gripped Peg by an arm.

"Let's get back to camp," he said gently. "We can eat the candy, and you can give Madeline the doll in the morning. Your friendship means a lot to me, Pegasus."

"Now you're talking hoss language," Peg agreed instantly. "And come to think of it, we ought not to leave the camp alone on account of the horses."

Back at the wagon, Pegasus built up the fire while Centaur King unwrapped the box of candy. Peg took three pieces and hunkered down on his boot-heels.

"Good," he murmured, as he chewed the sweets, and then he glanced beyond the circle of fire-light. "Someone coming, Centaur," he warned quietly.

"Howdy, men," a deep voice called, and Crag Tinsley came into the light with Madeline on his arm. She ran to Peg when the marshal set her down, and the boy held her at arm's length and showed her a piece of candy.

"Close your eyes, and open your mouth, Sugar Foots," he told the little girl.

Madeline giggled and closed her eyes. Then she opened her mouth wide, and Peg popped the candy between her rosy lips. He jerked around when another voice spoke.

"Can I close my eyes and open my mouth?"

Peg stared hard at Carol Tinsley and grunted. "Oh, it's you," he said, and held out the candy box to the girl.

"Yes, it's me, Peg," Carol said slowly. Then she closed her eyes and opened her mouth. She opened her eyes again when a piece of candy was popped into her mouth, but Peg was extending the box to the marshal.

"We were taking a little walk, and Madeline wanted to see her big brother," Crag Tinsley said with a chuckle. "Look, Pegasus," he continued, and now he was serious. "Why don't you stay here with us and finish up your schooling?"

Peg Bronte almost dropped the box of chocolates. "Who, me?" he demanded. "I done finished up with school, Marshal."

"You did?"

"Yeah, before I left Virginia. I went to school for eight years, Suh!"

"Hm," Tinsley murmured. "I guess that lets me out," he said quietly. "I got as far as the fifth grade, and then I went to punching cattle for old man Jim Teague."

"I couldn't leave Centaur nohow," Peg said earnestly. "It's like going to school you like, every day with Centaur. He teaches me a lot of things, and me and Centaur is going to California and mebbe up to Montanna."

"But not soon," Carol spoke up. "You have so much work to do here, and I want to make several sketches of you and Centaur."

"Hold me, Peg," Madeline demanded, and climbed into the boy's arms.

Peg put his arms around the little girl, but he was staring at Centaur King. He didn't say anything, but he had noticed instantly that the girl had called King by his first name.

"Had a little matter on my mind, King," the marshal spoke slowly. "You see, Carol and I have a nice little spread out in the valley. We're running mebbe some five hundred head of cattle critters, and if a man gave his time to it, he could easy enough run that many more. Thought mebbe you'd be interested in buying in and building up the spread."

Centaur King frowned thoughtfully and watched Peg Bronte's face. The boy was staring at him, and Peg shook his head one time. Only once, but the meaning was definite.

"That's right kind of you and Miss Carol," King answered slowly. "But you see, Crag, Peg and me like to travel, and we go where the work is."

"It gets in a man's blood," Peg Bronte spoke up, and now there was a dreamy, far away look in his dark eyes. "Always there's a horse or two that no one can handle. A man don't settle down to one place when he has the gift!"

Centaur King listened with a little smile tugging at his lips. He had said the same thing to Peg many times, and he was sure that Tinsley and his sister knew that Peg was merely repeating what he had heard an older person say.

"But you can't go away," a childish voice said tearfully. "You promised to be my big brother, Peggie, I mean Peg!"

"That there's better," Peg said gruffly, but his arms tightened around the tiny girl. "Brothers never stay to home noways," he told her. "They got too many things to do, and too many places to see."

"There's money to be made here," the marshal said to King. "Even if a man only stayed on the spread a part of the time, and tamed horses here and there when he heard about them."

"That's why we travel," King answered quietly. "It seems like a long time since I've beat the drum for Major Domo."

"You mean you will continue to be a showman?" Carol Tinsley asked. "You would walk down the main street of a town, playing that drum, with the black stallion prancing behind you?"

Centaur King turned to look at the girl, and then he nodded his dark head emphatically. "Yes," he answered quietly. "I will always be a showman, Miss Carol."

"What's wrong with that?" Peg Bronte demanded bluntly.

"Nothing; oh nothing," Carol answered, but her head was high. "Shall we go back now, Crag?" she asked her brother.

"It's about time, I reckon," the marshal answered heavily. "Madeline is getting sleepy. Well, bless my soul!"

He got up slowly, pointing to the little girl, Madeline was fast asleep, with her arms around Peg Bronte's neck. Peg looked down at the sleeping child and blushed with embarrassment.

"Well, I never did," the boy whispered. "Sugar Foots has done and gone fast asleep."

"She will miss you, feller," the marshal said gruffly. "Never saw her cotton to anyone else like that in all her life. She loves you, Peg; most as much as she does me."

He took the sleeping child gently, and Peg stood up. Centaur King was on his feet, with hat in hand, and he bowed as he told Carol Tinsley good-night.

Carol nodded with her head high, but she did not speak. When they were gone, Centaur King walked to the corral where Major Domo was penned. He stood there lost in thought until a small hand touched his arm.

"Did I say something wrong, Centaur?" Peg

asked anxiously. "The way Miss Carol acted and all?"

"You said it just right, pard," Centaur King answered with a smile. "I reckon it's just human nature for folks to want to change other folks."

"You mean Miss Carol would want you to stop beating the drum?" Peg asked with a frown.

"An artist travels to find material," King said quietly.

"Yeah, that's right, and Miss Carol is an artist," Peg murmured.

"I wasn't thinking of Miss Carol," King said gruffly. "Let's turn in and make up our sleep. We've work to do to-morrow!"

# CHAPTER SEVEN
## SOMETHING DIFFERENT

Dapper Jim Stacey came out of his little office near the gate of the sales ring. The monthly sale had been profitable, and his corrals were nearly empty. What horses remained were being trained by Centaur King and his young helper, and the auctioneer never tired of watching the two work.

Pegasus Bronte rode in on the golden stallion which was now broken to saddle, bridle-wise, and handled like a veteran. The boy called a cheery greeting to Stacey as he dismounted and began to strip his riding gear. Stacey sauntered over to the boarded pen where Marshal Crag Tinsley was watching Peg. He smiled as the boy talked to Tinsley like another man.

"Got Gold 'Un about ready for the road, Marshal. Course, he ain't trained to follow the drum as yet, but he's plenty smart and will learn fast."

"So you and Centaur won't change your minds about settling here in Lanthrope?" the marshal said hopefully, and he watched Peg's sensitive face.

"No, Suh," Peg answered frankly. "Just yester-day there was a cowhand rode through here from over Arizona way, and he was telling Centaur about a place over yonder where there were a lot of wild ones of oncommonly good breeding."

"Yeah, I know," Stacey interrupted. "And King began to get restless just hearing about those wild broncs. But what's this I hear about King buying up some of that hoss-trap land down the valley?"

"Did I hear someone mention my name?" a deep voice asked, and Centaur King came from behind the pen where he had been working with a slim-legged grey racer.

"Jim was asking about that piece of grazing land you were looking at down near my place," Tinsley made answer. "About two sections in that piece, if I remember right."

"Yeah, a little better than twelve hundred acres," King answered slowly. "I bought that piece," he told the two men, and Peg Bronte opened his mouth wide.

"You didn't tell me you bought it, pard," he said reproachfully.

"I just closed the deal last night," King explained with a twinkle in his eyes. "Only cost me a dollar an acre, and I traded two horses off in the bargain."

"Sounds right interesting," Tinsley remarked with a smile. "Once a man owns some of the good earth of Texas, we know he will always come back."

"You thinking of settling down?" Stacey asked

curiously, and Peg Bronte crowded closer to listen.

"Not exactly," King answered slowly. "You see, I pick up a good horse here and there I'd like to keep for experimental purposes. Then we see quite a few choice mares, and I've some ideas about short-coupled horses that can get away fast."

"You mean a breeding farm?" Stacey asked quickly.

"Something like that," King admitted. "Now you take a mare like Lady. She's got mighty fine blood lines, even if we don't know just what they are. I figured I could leave some bred mares graze in that pasture while Peg and me earn our living travelling about."

"Fine idea, Centaur," Stacey approved with enthusiasm. "You and Peg could come back here ever so often and work my sales. While you were here you could look after your own stock out in the valley."

"That's right," King agreed. "You see, Peg is half owner with me in this little deal, and I thought it would give him a sense of responsibility."

"Gee, Centaur, that's swell," the boy said happily, and then he turned to the marshal. "You be sure and tell Sugar Foots, won't you, Mister Tinsley, Suh? Tell her I'll be back often to see her."

"I'll tell her, Peg," the marshal assured the boy.

Peg whirled a hole in the dust with a toe of his boot. He glanced at Centaur King, looked over at the pen where the golden mare was corralled, and seemed uneasy. King smiled with understanding, and spoke confidently.

"Just get along with your work, Peg," he told the anxious boy. "Handle her gently but with firmness, and you better snub her to a post for this first go-around."

Stacey and Tinsley showed interest, but the auctioneer knew the language of horses. "You're going to work on Lady," he told Peg Bronte. "Unless I miss my guess, she's going to be a bit different than El Caballo Oro."

"I can handle her," Peg said quietly, and now his jaw was set in lines of determination.

"We've studied that mare," King told the two men. "She's going to come apart and buck like fury the first time out."

"Hadn't you better snap the rough out of her first?" Stacey asked dubiously.

King shook his head slowly. "I promised Pegasus that I'd stay out of it," he explained, but he was watching the boy get his gear ready. "He wants to go through all by himself with Lady, and I know just how he feels."

"She will throw him for a loss," Stacey stated, and his voice was a trifle harsh.

"She might," King admitted. "If she does, Peg will climb right back on her."

"He hasn't had enough seasoning," Tinsley added his bit. "He don't pack the weight for a bronc-busting job, and that mare is just out of the wild bunch!"

"I was riding the wild ones when I was sixteen," King said quietly. "It isn't only the riding, like we all know. I'll stand by if it will make you all feel any better, but the mare is Peg's affair. If he gives up on her, then I'll take over."

Peg Bronte was in the pen with the mare, slipping the light head-stall over her delicate ears. She balked some when he let down the bars, but the boy let her smell his left hand as he mumbled his queer horse-talk just above his breath. Then he led the mare into the ring and over to the snubbing post.

Taking an old soft rope, Peg Bronte slipped it about the mare's neck and tied a knot. One that he could undo quickly, but which would not draw tight and choke the mare if she fought the rope. Then he walked about the nervous animal, stroking her flanks and withers as he crooned in his throat.

The three men watched like poker players as Peg Bronte went about his preparations. The boy was wearing clean, neatly-pressed clothing. His white riding breeches were snugged down in English riding boots which shone like ebony. Crag Tinsley scratched his chin and tilted the unlighted cigar in the corner of his mouth.

"You and him," he said to King. "I never saw anything like you two in a breaking pen. You always wear clean clothes, while our bronc-stompers down this away wear the oldest rigging they can dig up."

"A horse reacts better to cleanliness," King said slowly. "Especially high-bred stock. And folks are a lot like horses that away, Marshal. Mebbe you don't know their parents, but you can always tell breeding where ever you see it. Peg Bronte will be a gentleman when he gets his growth, and he will be a man!"

"He has a good teacher," the marshal said gruffly. "Look at that mare rear up!"

The golden mare was rearing and clawing with her front feet. Peg Bronte stood back talking quietly, and then he stepped in and slapped the mare on the flank.

"Down, Lady! Down, I say!"

The mare thudded to earth and turned her head slowly to stare at the boy. He walked up and extended his hand, and she stretched out her neck and sniffed gingerly. But she settled down and became more quiet as he stroked her neck and talked in his unintelligible jargon.

Centaur King raised his head and removed his Stetson when he heard footsteps behind him. Carol Tinsley was coming into the yard, and the girl greeted King coolly.

"Good-morning, Mister King."

"Morning, Miss Carol," King answered politely. "Did you come to make a sketch this morning?"

"I did," the girl answered, and sat down on a little box. Then she seemed to see Peg Bronte and the golden mare for the first time, and two spots of colour leaped to her cheeks. "Is Pegasus going to attempt to ride Lady?" she asked King sharply.

"Peg is going to *ride* Lady," King corrected gently.

"I think you are cruel," the girl accused hotly.

"Please don't show excitement," King requested, and now his deep voice was firm. "We know our work as you know yours."

"But that mare might kill him," Carol Tinsley protested. "Are you just going to stand there, Crag?" she asked her brother.

"Yeah," the marshal answered bluntly. "He isn't breaking the law, and I never like for someone else to interfere with my business!"

Carol Tinsley tightened her lips as she placed a drawing pad on her knees and chose a soft pencil. Little tendrils of curly brown hair strayed from under the brim of her Creamy Stetson, and Centaur King watched the girl with a queer smile curling the corners of his mouth.

"If I were an artist, I'd like to sketch you now," he told the pouting girl.

"If you were an artist and a *man,* you'd be out there riding that wild mare!" the girl retorted acidly.

Centaur King's jaw tightened as he turned away. He walked away from the little group until he was just opposite Peg Bronte and the golden mare. Crag Tinsley spoke to his sister bluntly.

"You better stick to the work you know best, Carol," he suggested. "King knows what he's doing, and you don't!"

"He might be sending that boy to his death!" Carol retorted bitterly. "I've heard you say never to send a boy to do a man's work!"

"And I'd never send a girl to do a man's work," the marshal replied gruffly. Then his face changed as a little smile spread across his weathered face. "Centaur King bought those two sections adjoining our land," he said quietly.

Carol Tinsley jerked up her head, and her eyes widened. Her mouth opened with surprise, and then she closed it and set her lips grimly.

"I'm sure it does not interest me," she replied tartly, and made a few swift lines with her pencil.

Out in the ring, Peg Bronte was placing his saddle-blanket on the mare's back. She twitched her skin, but the boy talked soothingly and lifted his stock saddle. The mare kicked with her heels, and Peg lowered the saddle to the ground. Then he picked up a pair of rope hobbles and began to stroke the mare's front legs.

Centaur King watched without speaking. Peg fastened the hobbles to the front legs, passed a rope through the hobbles, and made fast to the snubbing post. Then he picked up his saddle again and laid it on the twitching back.

The mare kicked a time or two, but Peg Bronte kept on talking as he adjusted the saddle. He was some time tightening the latigo strap, but at last the saddle was firmly cinched in place. The rear cinch was not too tight, but the mare was going to be different from the golden stallion when it came to crawling the saddle.

Pegasus Bronte seemed to know this as he touched the left stirrup and judged how high he would have to make his little jump. He turned and looked at Centaur King, and the horse tamer crawled between the bars. Neither spoke, but both knew what was expected of them.

A man couldn't jump to the saddle and then throw off those hobbles. Centaur King did not touch the restive mare; neither did he add his voice to the crooning of Peg Bronte. He just stood by to do his part of the work, and Peg Bronte caught the left stirrup and made his jump.

The mare started forward and stopped when she felt the restraint of the hobbles. Peg Bronte set his boots in the oxbows, and nodded at King. The horse tamer ran a hand down the mare's left front leg, loosened the hobbles, and threw off the snubbing rope from the post.

And then it happened!

The golden mare swallowed her head and

started bawling. She kicked and clawed as she was bucking with her head low to the ground. Then she reared high and began to topple backward.

Like a flash, Peg Bronte pistoned out with the flat of his right hand between the laid-back ears. It saved both himself and the mare a bad fall, but now the maddened animal began to run.

Pegasus sat deep in the saddle with the light looped thong in his left hand. He tried to turn the infuriated mare, but she crashed into the bars blindly. Peg pulled up his left leg, and the mare bawled as she ducked her head between her front legs and kicked high behind.

Peg Bronte felt himself hurtling through space as his knee-lock was broken on the saddle. He landed hard in front of the pitching mare, rolled over twice in a cloud of dust, and came to his feet. He caught the trailing end of the tie-rope as the mare passed him, and then he hip-leaned against the rope with all his strength.

Carol Tinsley was on her feet now with her drawing pad clutched in her right hand. She gasped when Peg Bronte "busted" the mare. That is, he pulled her around, and stopped the mare so suddenly that the animal turned a hoolihan tail-over-head.

Centaur King was leaning against the rails watching intently. He made no move to help the boy who was moving in fast on the mare as she

106

struggled to her feet. When the mare surged up to her front feet, Peg Bronte hopped aboard and snubbed his boots deep in the carved wooden stirrups.

His dinky hat was in his right hand, and he began to slap the mare on the flanks. His heels beat a tattoo against her ribs, and the mare shook herself and started to buck. But now some of the steam had left her lungs, and Peg Bronte rose straight up and slick with a firm lock on the saddle.

"Come apart, and do yore wustest, you dad-burned jughead!" he shouted. "I can sit you from here to who pried the chunk, and all the way back. Yahoo, you wall-eyed wench!"

"That there's telling her!" Crag Tinsley roared. "Show that golden hussy who's the boss, Peg, ole bronc-stomper!"

The mare fence-cornered and then straightened up. Now Peg Bronte had stopped shouting and he was again crooning softly to the sweating mare. She raised her head, buck-jumped half-heartedly, and came to a stand.

Peg reached down and slapped her neck, nudged with a heel, and neck-reined to the left. The mare responded obediently, and Peg slid to the ground. For a time he stood under her head talking gently. His hands stroked the mare, and all the anger was gone from his thin face.

The mare listened with her head on his

shoulder. She nuzzled him playfully, and Peg Bronte turned the left stirrup and vaulted lightly to the saddle. After riding her around the ring, he reined over to the snubbing post and dismounted with a little jump.

Without bothering to even fasten the looped thong to the post, the boy loosened the latigo and allowed the cincha to drop free. Then he lifted his saddle, laid it aside with the skirts up to catch the air, and began to brush the sweating horse. She stood perfectly quiet under his gentle administrations, and Centaur King crawled back through the bars and walked up behind Carol Tinsley.

The girl was sketching rapidly, and King caught his breath. Carol had sketched the mare rearing high with Pegasus clinging to the saddle with his knees, his right hand upraised just about and between the mare's ears. The picture was done in bold rough strokes, but every bit of action and anatomy was perfect.

"Wonderful!" King murmured, just above his breath.

The girl whirled swiftly, and her eyes were flashing. "I can't say as much for you," she blazed at King. "Standing there while a little boy did your work!"

"I beg your pardon?"

"You should have worked the rough out of that mare first," Carol accused hotly. "Letting that boy get crashed against the fence, and then thrown the way he was!"

"But he rode her," Centaur King said quietly. "He will never have any trouble with that female of the species again!"

Carol Tinsley stopped sketching and turned to face King. She looked him up and down with evident distaste, and he returned her scrutiny with a little smile.

"You feel very superior, don't you?" she asked coldly.

"Do you?" he returned the question. "Telling me how to do my work?"

"Someone should tell you," the girl retorted, with a toss of her head.

"Perhaps, but you wouldn't be qualified," Centaur King answered politely. "Now I think your drawing is wonderful, and you have caught the whole splendid wild spirit of two natures conquesting. One of them had to be master; both dislike repression."

"I see," the girl answered with a twisted smile. "The male of the species had to be dominant!"

"It was, in this instance," King agreed.

"You haven't the courage of that boy!" the girl accused angrily.

Came a rush of boots across the ring, and Peg Bronte faced Carol Tinsley with his lips snarled back against his white teeth.

"You keep out of this, Ma'am!" he blazed at

Carol. "Me and Centaur don't need no female woman to tell us how to do our chores. Centaur offered to work Lady over for me, but I begged for the chance to learn some more of my lessons. You wouldn't talk like that to Centaur if you was a man!"

"Why . . . why I never!" the girl gasped.

"You did too," Peg accused angrily. "You did the same thing yesterday and the night before last. You curled yore lip up at Centaur on account of him beating the skins down the main street!"

"That will do, Pegasus," Centaur King said sternly. "You'll remember your manners, and do the needful, pard?"

Peg Bronte ground his teeth and his eyes flashed. His shoulders twitched nervously, and then he lowered his tousled head.

"I'm saying I'm sorry I spoke out of turn, Ma'am," he murmured, and whirling on one heel, he ran back to the golden mare which was whinnying softly.

"His manners are like those of a horse," Carol Tinsley told Centaur King. "I'm *saying* I'm sorry, not that he really was sorry."

"Honestly speaking, should he be?" King asked quietly.

"Lip service," the girl muttered.

"Social behaviour," King countered. "Most people don't say what they think, but in social circles, you always think before you say something."

"Are you trying to teach me manners?" the girl demanded.

Centaur King slowly shook his head. "No," he answered simply. "Perhaps I was just trying to justify the reactions of my young partner."

"He was cruel to Lady when he busted her!" the girl began on another tack.

"But now she loves him," King answered with a smile crinkling his eyes. "Mares are different from horses or stallions, but Peg is learning fast."

"I despise you, Centaur King," the girl said grimly.

King nodded and bowed from the hips. "I don't despise you, Miss Carol," he said gently. "Perhaps I pity you just a little," and he walked away to join Peg Bronte in the ring.

# CHAPTER EIGHT
## STAMPEDE

Twilight was deepening across the rolling Texas plains. The horse tamers were getting ready to break camp. Centaur King and Pegasus Bronte had spent a profitable two weeks in Lanthrope, during which time the neighbouring cattlemen on the big ranches had brought in their wildest horses.

King and the boy had talked of the horse spread they would operate some day, after Pegasus had served his apprenticeship, and had attained his full growth. Perhaps it would be on the two sections out in the valley, although Peg favoured California where high-bred horses were said to be more numerous.

Pegasus had tied up packs and had stored them in the big Conestoga wagon for an early start the following morning. Now the boy was cleaning up the supper dishes as Centaur talked to Dapper Jim Stacey who was urging the horse tamer to stay over in Lanthrope and go in business with him.

Peg saw King shake his head with a friendly smile. He could detect the restlessness of King, who wanted to be on the move. Pegasus also felt the same restlessness, though some of it had left him after the morning he had made his first ride on Lady.

"They won't ever fit Centaur to hobbles," the boy murmured to himself. "He'd stand for a while with tieing, but when he got ready to move on, Centaur would bust the stoutest rope they ever made."

Jim Stacey left the camp and went back to his little office near the auction corrals. When King came to the wagon, Pegasus spoke slowly in his soft drawl.

"Can't shake it off nohow, Centaur," Peg began haltingly. "I got a feeling that something is goin' to happen to we-uns."

Centaur King made no attempt to make light of the boy's premonition. He had felt the same unmistakable warning, and now he pointed to the two stallions tethered out on picket pins beyond the wagon.

"Something's in the wind, that's for certain," King agreed quietly. "Look at Major Domo, and Gold 'Un."

Pegasus turned to study the two stallions, then he dried his hands. Walking up to the golden stud, the boy patted the sleek neck with gentle hands. The big stallion threw up his head, facing the south with ears pricked forward.

"It's hosses, Centaur," Pegasus said to King. "Wild ones from the look of Gold 'Un. I'm going to tie them up short, one to each back wheel of the wagon, just to make for sure."

"We won't have to worry about the mares we took down to our little hoss-trap in the valley," King said thoughtfully. "Lady should have a beautiful foal next year, and you will be started in business."

Pegasus nodded, though he felt a little tug at his heart. He missed the golden mare, but she would have company. A dozen other selected mares had been bred to Major Domo and El Caballo Oro, and the feed was plentiful on the two sections of valley land.

Crag Tinsley had promised to keep an eye on the brood mares, and little Madeline had made quite a scene when she had bade Pegasus a tearful farewell. Pegasus wondered about Carol Tinsley, but he said nothing about her absence, and Centaur King seemed relieved.

"I'm going to miss Sugar Foots," Pegasus murmured in the golden stallion's ear. "But me and Centaur don't want no truck with women, and that's what ever!"

"What say?" King called from the wagon.

"Just tellin' Gold 'Un we will be back some day to see Lady," Pegasus answered, with his face turned away. He wasn't much of a hand at telling falsehoods, and Pegasus knew that Centaur King could detect the guilty flush on his face if he could see it.

"Better bring the horses over and call it a day," King suggested. "It will feel good to be on the move again, and my hands are itching to roll the drumsticks."

"Yeah," Pegasus agreed heartily. "And we can teach Gold 'Un to prance and rattle like Major Domo does it."

The twilight faded and dusk stole over the plains as Pegasus finished his chores. He tied the two stallions to the wagon, threw them a forkful of prairie hay, after which he banked the fire and rolled his blankets under the wagon between the hind wheels. Pegasus wrinkled his nose to inhale the familiar smells of horses and hay, wagon grease, and wood smoke. Then he sighed and was instantly asleep.

Centaur King was sleeping in the wagon when he heard the black stallion snort. Pegasus Bronte awoke instantly, and called softly to Major Domo. He had gone to bed "Standing up" by merely pulling off his jockey boots, and then the golden stallion snorted with alarm. Peg Bronte reached in the wagon and shook King, calling in a guarded voice so as not to spook the horses.

"Pull yore britches on and come a-runnin', Centaur. Hosses on the loose, and comin' this away fast!"

Centaur King dressed quickly and jumped to the ground. Peg Bronte had the two stallions saddled and bridled, and both animals were now snorting with excitement. A low rumbling roar was audible and growing louder, as Pegasus leaped to his saddle on the golden stallion.

"She's a stampede, Centaur!" the boy shouted above the roar of pounding hooves. "They'll be here at almost any minute!"

"I had a feeling," King answered, and he climbed the saddle on Major Domo. "We better ride these stallions into Stacey's pens for safe-keeping, or they will take off with the wild bunch!"

"I put the team in stalls," Pegasus shouted. "We won't have time to make the change now. Here they come, Centaur!"

Before the two riders could cross the clearing to the auction corrals, all perdition came in from the west. A thundering band of stampeding horses roared out of the darkness and on through the camp. Centaur King was on the left side of the wagon, holding Major Domo in check with a firm hand, but he heard a scream as the golden stallion was swept away by the rush of the stampede.

King centered around and watched the skyline. He was about to start in pursuit when he made out the slight figure of Pegasus Bronte etched against the eastern sky. Then King saw a second rider on a blocky horse which seemed vaguely familiar. As the scream of maddened rage shattered the night air, Centaur King recognized the stocky horse beyond a doubt.

It was Sam Bailey's bay gelding which had eaten the roots of loco weed!

Caught up in the mad rush of the stampede, Pegasus Bronte went along with the flood on the golden stallion. The boy tried to crowd over to the outer edge, and he was making some progress. Suddenly a big horse loomed up out of the dark and lunged into the stallion, almost knocking El Caballo Oro from his feet.

Peg steadied the stallion and sucked in his breath sharply. A big man was riding the horse which had lunged into Gold 'Un, and the man was riding hard and coming in again at a slant.

The golden stallion snorted and bunched up his muscular flanks. The stallion seemed to sense that the bay gelding was crazy, and now the gelding's blood was running hot just as Centaur King had explained it to his pupil.

Blind anger swept over Pegasus Bronte as he realized that Sam Bailey had deliberately planned the stampede. He reached down with his left hand and gripped the neck of the golden stallion near the white flowing mane. If he could get Gold 'Un in the clear for a scant second, he would turn the big stallion against the crazed bay, and El Caballo Oro would do the rest.

Gold 'Un had been a range stallion, and he would fight like a wild monarch. Heels or clawing front hooves, or great snapping teeth, he would use every weapon to kill off the attacker.

But Sam Bailey was as crazed as the locoed horse he was straddling, and he saw the boy's intention. He crowded the bay in close, spurring with both cruel rowels, and his right fist shot out to clip Peg Bronte viciously on the right shoulder near the neck.

The boy was nearly torn from the saddle as the driving blow paralyzed the muscles in his upper arm. A sickening sensation of nausea swept over him, and Peg Bronte drooped in the saddle. Then the scudding clouds rifted with a sickle moon lighting up the course of the terrific stampede.

Pegasus clutched the saddle-horn with his left hand and hung on desperately. He had to hand and rattle until help reached him, and he saw the help coming up fast on a big black stallion as Centaur King located Sam Bailey.

King was on the outside of the band, riding like a Cossack. Half a dozen horses separated him from Bailey, who was bringing back his right fist to drive the finishing blow against his helpless victim.

Centaur King whispered a cowboy's prayer as he wished for the gun he seldom wore. But there were other tools of the trade, and King grabbed his coiled rope from the pommel on the left side of the saddle-horn.

His slender fingers fashioned a loop even as he whirled the catch-rope over his head to spread the noose. Centaur King shot the loop across the backs of the running horses like a bullet. The noose dropped over Bailey's head, pinned his arms to stop the blow he was just driving at Peg Bronte, and before Bailey could catch his balance, he was dragged from his saddle and back over the cantle.

Pegasus Bronte saw the big man slide down between two racing horses and disappear. The bay kept pressing in, but now Centaur King was wedging a way between the leaders. The golden stallion was still slanting outward, with other horses preventing his escape from the crazed bay. Then Centaur King was on the other side of the locoed horse.

It happened so quickly that Pegasus did not see Centaur King make his leap and change from the black stallion to the saddle bay. But there he was, trying to ease the bay away from El Caballo Oro, and the boy began to breathe easier.

This was something different from a short fast ride where the rider could control his horse and rein to a stop when he had had enough. The stampeding horses would run until they were exhausted, taking out fences which blocked their way, or tromping anything which fell under their thundering hooves.

Pegasus turned slightly to watch Centaur King who was fighting the bay. Now King held the bay steady as he began to mutter with his lips close to the ear of the maddened brute. His left hand went down and began to stroke the sweating neck, and the black stallion began to slow the pace, running close to his master on the blocky bay.

Peg Bronte also slowed the golden stallion some, and the circulation was beginning to return to his numbed arm. The clouds had lifted, and the sickle moon cast a pale silvery light over the vast unbroken prairie. Peg turned his head and watched the face of Centaur King, and now the horse tamer's black eyes were glowing like hooded rubies.

Pegasus Bronte again felt that awe which always came to him when he was witnessing a new trick of the master. King's eyes were like those of a night animal, and the light in them resembled fox-fire.

The bay was running easily now, and the streamers of froth were no longer ringing its flaring nostrils. The animal was quiet under the gentle pressure of King's right hand, and the stampede was slowing down to a trot. A moment later the band was walking behind the three saddled horses. Not until then did Centaur King speak to the boy.

"Are you hurt, Peg?" he asked anxiously, as he laid his right hand on the boy's arm.

Pegasus Bronte could feel the powerful vibrations from Centaur King's fingers, and then he knew why the wild horses always obeyed the master's touch. His own pulses slowed down as his blood began to cool, and he felt a new and tremendous confidence in himself.

"I'm not hurt none to speak of, Centaur," Peg answered quietly. "I wasn't afraid for myself, but Sam Bailey was makin' that locoed bay run down Gold 'Un, and us on a slant."

"Start swinging over to the left," Centaur King said quietly. "The bay will be right beside you, and Major Domo will press right in close. We'll start this hoss-band back toward Lanthrope, and when we get them strung out, you drop back slowly and bring up the drag."

Peg Bronte neck-reined slightly to the left to start a wide circle. The weary horses followed without hesitation, and after a time, Peg straightened out the golden stallion. Now they were headed back toward town, and the boy gradually dropped back as Centaur King took the lead on the bay gelding.

Major Domo was trotting beside the bay with his grand head held high. The bay gelding was under control, and except for dripping with sweat, seemed none the worse for his wild run through the night.

An hour later, Centaur King rode through the streets of Lanthrope at the head of the wild horse-band. Men were riding around the corrals behind Dapper Jim Stacey's auction ring, and King led his band right through the wide gates.

Stacey's hostlers were manning the pen gates,

and after King had ridden through, they closed the barred gates and penned the weary band. Stacey met Centaur King and gripped the horse tamer's hand.

"We thought you and Pegasus were run down," the auctioneer said shakily, and he was breathing hard like a man who had run a great distance. "How in time did you stop that stampede, and how did you get 'em turned out there in the dark?"

"The two stallions did the work," King answered quietly and his voice was calm and controlled. "Sam Bailey tried to kill Pegasus, and I roped that killer out of the saddle!"

"I know," Stacey said, nodding his head. "The marshal just brought Sam Bailey in. Found him out on the prairie a-foot."

Centaur King straightened a trifle as Pegasus Bronte rode around and stood the golden stallion close to Major Domo. It was King who asked the question in a low voice.

"Was Bailey—dead?"

Stacey made no answer. He turned and pointed to the Conestoga wagon under the cottonwood trees. Two big men were standing near the wagon in the moonlight, and even Centaur King did not believe what he saw. One of the men was Marshal Crag Tinsley; the other was Sam Bailey.

"He was just jolted some," Stacey murmured. "Only the good die young. Crag wants you and the button to ride over and talk some!"

"Talk, and what's to say?" King asked slowly, and Pegasus turned his head to follow the direction of King's dark eyes. Pegasus sucked in his breath and grunted when he saw Carol Tinsley seated near the grub box, but the boy trapped his lips together and did not speak.

Centaur King turned the bay over to Stacey and mounted the black stallion. He rode over to the wagon and swung down near the marshal and his hulking prisoner.

"I went loco, King," Sam Bailey spoke up hurriedly. "Got to fighting my head, and I'm willing to pay the damage!"

"You sign the complaint, and I'll see that this hombre gets the limit," Crag Tinsley told King grimly. "He's a killer by nature, and mean to boot!"

"You meant to kill the best friend a man ever had," Centaur King told Bailey quietly. "You hit a half-grown boy, and you tried to run him down with a crazy horse!"

"And I nearly got killed, and serve me right," Bailey said humbly. "If you hadn't dropped the end of your rope, I'd have been dragged to death by that locoed bay. They ain't much I can say."

"I told you not to run the bay," King said sternly. "You knew what would happen if his blood got hot!"

"Come down to the calabozo and sign the complaint," the marshal urged. "This hombre will have a long time to think about the error of his ways."

"I'll give you a clean Bill of Sale for that band of wild hosses," Bailey spoke up hopefully. "Most of 'em are mares, and if that won't pay the damage, just name your own figger. I'll pay anything you say, but I'm asking you not to send me to prison if you can see your way to let me off. I'd die shut away from the sun, and I've learned a lesson I'll remember the rest of my life. I'm promising you that, Centaur King!"

Pegasus Bronte listened and turned his head away. He knew the gentleness of Centaur King; knew also the inflexible will of the man when aroused. He did not want to see that terrible light in King's eyes, and Pegasus gasped slightly when he heard Centaur King make his answer.

"I'm not signing any complaint, Marshal." Then King turned to Bailey. "You meant to kill Pegasus Bronte and his golden stallion," he said sternly. "Just make out the Bill of Sale to him. Now Pegasus really is in the hoss business, and you're lucky he didn't get hurt too much!"

"Thanks, and I was out of my head," Bailey murmured gratefully. Then he took a paper from his pocket. "I'll make it out to the button," he agreed. "I'll pay him ten thousand dollars to get him set up in business!"

"You won't!" King contradicted sternly. "The horses will be enough, but I'd have killed you with my hands if Pegasus had slipped from the saddle out in that stampede!"

Pegasus heard someone draw breath in sharply. He turned to glance at Carol Tinsley, and the girl was staring at Centaur King with something like horror mirrored in her wide eyes. Pegasus sniffed unconsciously, and then he glared at the girl when Carol Tinsley looked up and saw him watching her.

"I promise never to make you any more trouble," Sam Bailey told King earnestly.

"Trouble?" Centaur King repeated, and then he smiled slowly. "You didn't make me any trouble I couldn't handle, Bailey. You did just what I asked you to do the day I rode into town. I asked you and the others traders and cattlemen to do me a favour, and you did it. Remember, Bailey? I asked you to—bring me wild horses!"

# CHAPTER NINE
## STAND AND DELIVER

Carol Tinsley coughed suggestively as Centaur King led Major Domo to the wagon and tied the black stallion to a rear wheel. The horse tamer straightened slowly when he had made his knot. Then he faced the girl with Stetson in his hand, and bowed slightly.

"Howdy, Miss Carol," he said quietly. "Haven't seen you for quite some time."

"We've both been so busy," the girl answered and her voice sounded warm and friendly. "You were going away without telling me good-bye," she accused.

"Yes," King admitted frankly. "I thought you wanted it that way."

"Ships that pass in the night," Carol quoted. "But then, I knew you would come back to port, because of the land down in the valley."

"An anchor to windward," King agreed. "If I should change my mind, it will always mean a good start for Pegasus."

Carol Tinsley bit her lower lip, and then she sighed. "I know how much you think of Pegasus," she murmured. "Do you know there are really two of you, Centaur King?" she asked thoughtfully.

"One of me is enough," King said carelessly, but he eyed the girl closely. "What do you mean?" he asked curiously.

"There's Centaur King, the master, and Centaur King, loyal friend," Carol explained her thought. "You are a mixture of many things, Mister King. I saw killer light in your eyes as you told Sam Bailey . . ."

"I meant what I said," King answered coldly. "If serious harm had come to Pegasus, I'd have killed Sam Bailey with these two hands!"

He held up his strong, long-fingered hands, and Carol Tinsley shuddered. The marshal had walked away with Sam Bailey, and Pegasus was picking up around the camp.

"I like the other King best," the girl said slowly. "When you show your great love for horses, you are of your best. I don't like you so well when you demonstrate your dominance."

"No one likes to be dominated," Centaur King agreed bluntly, and then he stopped speaking. His silence after the statement was more eloquent than any argument or counted accusation, and Carol Tinsley felt the flush that warmed her cheeks.

"Perhaps I don't understand what you mean," she said hesitantly.

"And perhaps you do," King answered. "Thinking one thing, and saying another, is one of the social graces I do not cultivate!"

"I beg your pardon?"

"Granted, but honest understanding begins in the heart," King said softly.

Carol Tinsley set her little jaw and rose to her feet. She studied King's stern face for a long moment, forgetting the strain he had been under during the mad stampede.

"Good-bye, Mister King, and I wish you luck," she said, and her voice was very formal.

"Likewise," King answered quietly. "*Adios*, Miss Carol."

Pegasus heard the final greeting, and when Carol Tinsley had walked to the little office, the boy leaped into the air, cracked the heels of his boots together, and danced a little jig. Centaur King stared at the antics without smiling.

"Did you brush Golden down good?" he asked a trifle sharply.

"I brushed both them studs down, Centaur," the boy answered. "They'll be ready to travel at daybreak, and I never felt better in my whole life!"

"That will do!" King said gruffly.

"Did I say something out of the way?" Pegasus asked innocently.

Centaur King picked up a short length of rope and doubled it in his right hand. He stared at the boy with speculation in his dark eyes, and Pegasus came closer.

"Lay it on if it will make you feel any better,

Centaur," he said slowly. "You deserve the best in the world, and up to now you've always wanted the best!"

"I still want the best," King burst out, and his voice sounded savage with restraint.

"Yes, Suh," Pegasus agreed, and then he closed his lips tightly.

Centaur King stared moodily for a time, threw the rope aside, and thwacked Pegasus across the shoulders.

"You're good to teach a feller self-control, pard," he said quietly. "I'll go over and ask Jim Stacey to haze that band of hosses down to our valley land, and we'll start rolling with the dawn. Now you better turn in and make up some sleep. And Peg?"

"Yeah, Centaur."

"Don't go out of your way saying things to rile me up, huh?"

Peg Bronte did not resort to the childish artifice of injured innocence, and he wanted no part of subterfuge.

"I'll remember, Centaur," he promised gravely. "And here's my hand on it!"

The two shook hands in the waning moonlight, and King walked away to see Dapper Jim Stacey. Pegasus watched him go, and then he murmured softly just above his breath.

"I'd die for Centaur, and I want him to have the best!"

130

King stopped near the little office when he saw two figures walking slowly up the street. He could recognize Dapper Jim because of the cutaway checkered coat, and the girl with Stacey would be Carol Tinsley. He had forgotten that she had gone to Stacey's office, and King entered the little building and left a note for the auctioneer. Asking him to have his men drive the horse-band down to the valley pasture, and saying that he would see Stacey again soon.

Pegasus was asleep in his bedroll under the wagon when King came back to the fire. The embers were glowing richly, and the horse tamer stared at the coals. Something had gone out of his life; something which he had not as yet put into conscious thought.

All his life Centaur King had been searching for something, with a restlessness which had kept him constantly on the move. It wasn't something a man could put a name to, when he didn't know what it was that he sought.

After a time King straightened slowly, and his dark eyes glowed with a strange light of understanding. That was it, he told himself silently. He was discontented, and the thing for which he sought was . . . *content!*

It wasn't something a man could buy with money; Centaur King had enough of that, and to spare. The Shah of Persia had paid him a fee of five thousand dollars for gentling one horse.

Other wealthy men had been equally as prodigal; his last trip abroad had netted more than a hundred thousand.

There was his horse farm back in Kentucky in the heart of the Blue Grass country, and the money in a dozen different banks. He had worked diligently at his trade for more than a dozen profitable years, and his habits and wants were simple.

Some of the discontent had left him since Pegasus Bronte had attached himself to Centaur King. He had met many women, but he had always felt strangely unresponsive. At the slightest sign of possessiveness, Centaur King admitted honestly to himself that he preferred the open road, and the lure of far-away places.

That was the answer, he told himself with vehement finality. He and Pegasus would start for California, and perhaps Montana and Idaho. Where they raised strong men and big horses; big *wild* horses.

Centaur King smiled dreamily and climbed into the wagon. He removed his boots and Stetson, crawled into his bunk, and was almost instantly asleep. And when the first vagrant fingers of dawn tugged at his eyelids, King threw back his blankets and pulled on his boots.

Pegasus heard the thud of boots on the floor of the Conestoga wagon, and he greeted King with a cheerful smile as he rolled from his bed. King returned the smile and said he would get the team ready while Peg prepared breakfast, and neither mentioned their conversation of the previous night.

They rolled out of Lanthrope before the town was out of bed, with Peg Bronte in the driver's seat, and Centaur King sitting beside him. The two stallions were tied to the tail-gate, and King hummed a little song in a rich baritone voice as the wagon wheels rolled westward.

Peg Bronte was like a different boy as he handled the leather on the spanking team of bays. He hummed along with King in an off-key harmony which brought a smile to the horse tamer's tanned face. Peg said that this was the life for him, and there was no doubting his sincerity. His face glowed with happiness, and with something far deeper when he glanced sideways at the man on the seat beside him.

"What's the next town we play, Centaur?" Peg asked curiously. "I hope it's not too close."

"Little town by the name of Stanhope," King answered lazily. "Not as prosperous as Lanthrope, but there's plenty of big ranches nearby, and that means work for us. It's about thirty miles from Lanthrope, and we're about halfway there now."

The dirt road made a bend to avoid a low rock hill, and the wagon rolled along through high brush which fringed the road and told of water nearby. They reached a ford in a shallow creek, where Peg stopped the team to drink. He leaned back against the seat, glanced carelessly at King, and jerked erect.

"Sit still!" King whispered, barely moving his lips. "It's a hold-up!"

"Stand and deliver!" a gruff voice commanded. "We need money and fresh hosses, and here's where we get both!"

Pegasus gasped and jerked his eyes to the speaker at the side of the road in the brush. He saw a bearded face with a bandanna covering the lower part, and the blued barrel of a six-shooter in the bandit's grimy hand. Peg looked to the right, and saw another ruffian watching him over a cocked six-shooter.

"Money, yes," Centaur King said calmly. "Horses . . . no!"

"Step down, you and the button," the first bandit ordered hoarsely. "Make a play for a hide-out gun, and I'll salivate you through the ticker!"

"You're the boss," King answered quietly, and climbed down over the wheel. Peg Bronte fastened his reins to the whipstock, and climbed down the off-side wheel with his hands above his head.

"Shell out, or we search the wagon," the first outlaw barked.

Centaur King slowly reached to the inside pocket of his coat. He saw the bandit's jaw tighten, and King kept his hand inside his coat.

"I have no gun on me," the horse tamer said quietly. "Do you want my wallet, or not?"

"Bring that grub-hook out slow, Dude," the bandit warned. "If you're holding Sixes full, you won't get a shot away. I said . . . *slow!*"

"Slow it is," King repeated, and withdrew his hand until the bandit could see the leather wallet.

"Toss that leather yere!" the bandit snapped. "Then you reach for sky and stand hitched!"

Centaur King tossed his wallet to the bandit and raised both hands above his head. The outlaw caught the wallet, opened it eagerly, and shouted at his companion.

"Five or six hundred here, Pete! Never mind searching the wagon. Ride back there and get those two hosses while I keep these Pilgrims covered!"

"Not the horses!" Centaur King contradicted quietly.

"I'm giving the orders around here!" the outlaw shouted. "I'll take that black, and you change your gear to the claybank, Pete!"

"Don't you lay a hand on Gold 'Un," Peg Bronte warned in a low tense whisper. "You do, I'll pass him the word to kill yore pard!"

"Pay that button no mind, Peter," the first outlaw sneered. "We take what we want, and we don't want any of your slack jaw!"

"Steady, Peg," King warned the boy softly. "Never argue with a loaded gun!"

135

"Say, you've got sense for a dude," the bandit told King. "Hurry up with those hosses, Pete!"

The second bandit was stripping the riding gear from his sweating horse. He approached the golden stallion, flapped his saddle-blanket on the palomino's back, and the horse lunged to the side. Then El Caballo Oro reared high and threw himself backward, and the rope broke near the halter.

Peg Bronte heard the uproar and faced around to see what was happening. He saw the golden stallion race away down the back trail, and the bandit called Pete swore viciously as he drew his six-shooter. Pegasus screamed when the heavy pistol roared, but again Centaur King cautioned softly.

"Easy, Peg. It would take an expert to hit that golden stud, and he's out of range now!"

"Gone!" Peg murmured brokenly. "Gold 'Un has left me!"

The first bandit spoke harshly as he centered his gun on King. "That black yore personal hoss?"

"That's right," King answered promptly.

"You think a heap of him?"

"More than that," King said. "Tell Pete not to touch Major Domo!"

"You Pete, don't touch that black stud," the bandit called, and then he leered at King. "All right, Mister," he said quietly. "Shag on back there and get that black. Lead him up here, and change my saddle. You give me any trouble, I'll shoot the hoss first!"

Centaur King stiffened, thought a moment, and nodded his head. He walked to the rear of the wagon, spoke softly to the black stallion, and untied the rope. Then he led the horse up front and ground tied him by throwing the rope to the earth.

The bandit dismounted without losing the drop. Centaur King loosed the heavy saddle, spoke softly to Major Domo, and made the change. The man named Pete was re-saddling his horse, and he rode up front to watch his partner.

"Cover these two, Pete," the first bandit told his partner. "I never saw the hoss yet I couldn't tame, and this black devil won't be any different!"

"Don't abuse him," King said quietly. "He will carry you, but if you cut him up, he will kill you!"

The first bandit was a heavy man with wide shoulders, thick through the middle, and nearly six feet tall. He was also a good horseman, and he was in the saddle as soon as the cincha was tightened.

Major Domo grunted and took a step toward Centaur King. The horse tamer lowered his hands, stroked the black muzzle, and spoke softly.

"Easy, boy. I'll be seeing you!"

"Mebbe I ought to change to one of those bays in the team," Pete suggested.

"We've lost enough time already," the big

bandit growled. "Hit on out, and we'll pick up a fresh horse later."

He touched Major Domo with a spur, and the black stallion leaped into a dead run. The second bandit was leading the horse his partner had ridden, and Pegasus stared at Centaur King with a stricken look in his dark eyes.

"Gold 'Un, and now Major Domo," he whispered, and his chin quivered.

"Head up!" King said gently, and then he put the index fingers of both hands between his lips. King drew a deep breath, and a high almost soundless whistle keened from his lips.

The bandits were almost to the bend of the road when Centaur King blew his shrill high blast. Major Domo jerked up his head, and the bandit hit the stallion hard with the spurs. King blew another keen blast, and the stallion whirled swiftly and then started to buck.

The bearded outlaw grabbed the saddle-horn and spurred with both feet. The black stallion started a rush, deliberately swallowed his head, and crashed down in a complete somersault before the bandit could kick his boots free.

Centaur King was already in action. He ran swiftly to the back of the wagon and vaulted inside. His hand opened a drawer, and drew out a long-barrelled duelling pistol. Then King leaped to the ground just as Major Domo raced up to the wagon.

"Steady, boy!" King commanded. "Easy, I say!"

The stallion pranced away and circled in front of the team. The second bandit was racing back with his six-shooter in his right hand. He triggered a shot at Centaur King who was bringing the duelling pistol up to meet his eye.

The bandit's bullet whistled into the wagon just above King's head. Then the gun spoke sharply in his steady hand, and the bandit screamed and toppled from his horse.

"Got him!" Peg Bronte whispered hoarsely. "You killed him, Centaur!"

Centaur King nodded, and some of the stern harshness left his thin face. He walked slowly forward and stopped to stare at the bandit named Pete. A banner of crimson was flagging out on the dead man's grimy shirt, just over the heart. Centaur King sighed and continued on until he reached the man who had stolen Major Domo. Pegasus Bronte ran up and stood beside the horse tamer.

"His neck is all crooked, Centaur," the boy whispered. "You reckon . . . ?"

"Yes," King answered quietly. "Major Domo risked his own neck to return to me, and he broke this outlaw's neck!"

"Gee, I'm scared," Pegasus whispered. "Two dead men!"

"Dead men won't ever hurt you, Peg," King

said heavily. "I'm sorry about Gold 'Un, but perhaps he will come back. I'm sure he will, if you love him enough," he added.

Peg Bronte turned slowly and then ran back to the wagon. He threw himself over the tail-gate, crept into his bunk, and sobbed without restraint.

Centaur King nodded and walked slowly past the wagon to the team. He called softly, and the black stallion minced up and nuzzled his shoulder. King unsaddled the stallion and threw the gear beside the road. Then he led Major Domo to the rear and fastened the stallion to the tail-gate. He could hear Pegasus sobbing as he climbed to the driver's seat and picked up the leather ribbons.

"Yup," he said to the team. "We'll have to make a report to the law in Stanhope!"

# CHAPTER TEN
## FULLY DRESSED

Centaur King was moody as he drove along the little-used road to Stanhope. He was thinking over the conversation he had held with Carol Tinsley, in which the girl had pointed out that he was two different men. He felt a certain regret for the man he had been forced to kill in self-defence. For the bandit who had tried to steal Major Domo he had no feeling.

All was quiet in the back of the wagon, but King knew how Pegasus Bronte felt. The boy had given his heart to El Caballo Oro, and now the golden stallion had returned to the wild bunch in the distant southern hills. King stopped the bay team when he heard the patter of boots which warned him that Pegasus was coming forward to ride on the seat.

Pegasus climbed over the left wheel and tried to smile at King. The team started up, and Peg Bronte began to talk.

"I've been thinking, Centaur," he said soberly, in the tone he always used. Man to man, or as equals. "I've been thinking about what I'd do if I was a hoss like Gold 'Un."

King nodded his understanding and remained

silent to hear what the boy had thought out. Peg Bronte was staring off into space with his brow furrowed. His voice was a slow drawl as he talked to the horse tamer.

"I'm a wild hoss," Peg began. "I was caught when I was a yearling. Now I'm four years old, and saddle-broke. I ran with the wild bunch in a stampede, and those wild mares are back up the trail. Now I'm free again, so I'll just high-tail and look up that band of mares!"

Centaur King sat up straight and then stopped the team. "Say!" he ejaculated. "Sounds like good hoss sense to me. Tell you what we'll do, Peg. We'll camp right along here when we come to the next water, and make camp for the night. Then we'll wheel around and back-track to-morrow. A day or two won't make any difference, and you just might be right!"

"Thanks, Centaur," Peg Bronte said simply, but he gripped King's forearm to tell of his appreciation.

King was about to start the team again when the thud of shod hooves announced the coming of horse-backers. Then six men came galloping around the west bend of the road, all armed with six-shooters and saddle-guns. The leader wore a bright five-pointed star on his vest, and he reined in his horse when he saw the wagon.

"Howdy, stranger," he greeted King. "I'm Sheriff Clay from Stanhope. These men are my posse, and we're looking for two desperate outlaws. Both wore beards, and the law wants those two mighty bad. Seen anything of a pair like that?"

"Yes, Sheriff," King answered quietly. "My name is Centaur King, and this is Pegasus Bronte, my helper."

"You're the hoss tamer," the sheriff said promptly. "We heard about you from Lanthrope; heard you were heading your way to Stanhope. You say you saw Pete Powers and Al Johnson, those outlaws I mentioned?"

King nodded soberly. "Both dead," he said, and his deep voice sounded harsh. "They held us up back aways," he explained, and then he told the sheriff the whole story.

Sheriff Clay listened intently until the report was finished. The men in his posse slid their thirty guns into the saddle-scabbards with something of disappointment.

"There's a reward of a thousand apiece on those two killers," the sheriff told King. "I'll see that you get it. And say, did you search those two?"

King shook his dark head. "I just recovered my wallet," he answered quietly. "We are going back to Lanthrope to hunt for the golden stallion, and you'll find those two along the road by the next creek. The one you called Johnson has a broken neck."

"We'll wait for you at the creek," the sheriff

said, and ordered his posse ahead with a wave of his arm.

Centaur King turned his team and started back toward Lanthrope. When they reached the creek and crossed the ford where the hold-up had taken place, they saw the sheriff and his posse near the bodies of the dead men. Sheriff Clay shouted for King to stop his team and come over for a talk.

"You pull off the road on that little flat and unspan the horses," King told Peg Bronte. "We'll camp here for the night."

Pegasus nodded and took the driver's seat as King jumped to the ground. The posse had caught the two weary horses, and Al Johnson's saddle was lying on the grass. King widened his eyes when he saw the saddle-bags which had been dumped on the grass.

"Money," King said slowly. "Looks like they might have robbed a bank."

"That's right," Sheriff Clay agreed. "They robbed the Drovers Bank in Stanhope, killed two men, and escaped with eight thousand. Every dollar of it was right in those saddle-bags, thanks to you, Centaur King!"

"I'm glad you recovered the loot," King answered, and his voice was low, and a bit tired.

"Banker Jud Stebbins offered a reward of twenty-five hundred for the recovery of the money," the sheriff stated. "You've earned it, King."

Centaur King frowned and shook his head. "I don't want blood money," he said bluntly. "Is there a fund for the widows of peace officers, Sheriff?"

"Why, yes, there is," the sheriff answered slowly.

"Just give those rewards to the fund," Centaur King told Clay. "I earn mine taming wild horses!"

"Just as you say, Mr. King, and thank you," the sheriff accepted gratefully. "One of the men killed was my deputy, and his wife is expecting a child. If there is anything we can do to help you, just you say the word!"

"In case Pegasus was wrong, you might keep your eyes open for that golden stallion," King said eagerly. "He bought that stallion in Lanthrope with his savings, and he's heartbroken about losing Gold 'Un!"

"We'll get up a bunch and search the hills for that stud," the sheriff promised. "But right now we've got to take these remains back to Stanhope. Don't you carry a belt-gun, King?"

Centaur King shook his head slowly. "Not often," he replied.

"You should, on the road," the sheriff suggested. "I'd say you got Powers at better than forty yards, and that's mighty good shooting!"

Centaur King reached to the inside pocket of his coat and produced the duelling pistol.

145

He handed it to the sheriff who examined the beautiful weapon with interest.

"Say!" Clay spoke jerkily. "This pistol has a royal crest on it. British, unless I'm wrong."

"I have a pair," King explained. "I gentled a stallion for a man in England, and he presented me with the pistols!"

"I remember now," the sheriff said positively, and he studied King's face with a new respect. "That man in England was the Prince of Wales," he stated. "I saw the piece in the paper."

"Well, I'll be helping Peg with the chores," King said, and it was evident that he was uncomfortable. He walked slowly away from the road, and the boy looked up from the fire he was building.

"Did the law take your gun?" he asked King.

King smiled and took the pistol from his pocket. "I just showed it to the sheriff," he answered. "Now I must clean the weapon, and put it away again."

Pegasus watched while King broke down the duelling pistol and carefully cleaned the beautiful weapon. The sheriff's posse was lifting the bodies of the dead men to their horses, lashing ankles and wrists together, and Sheriff Clay rode up to the wagon. He carried a shell-studded belt on his left arm, and he swung the belt to King who caught it with his left hand.

"Al Johnson won't need that hardware any

more, and you better strap it on," Clay said shortly. "It's a good Colt forty-five, and I'd like for you to keep this gun!"

"Thanks, Sheriff," King murmured, and slipping the gun from the holster, he examined it curiously. "Five notches whittled on the handles," he said slowly.

"Johnson was a cold killer," the sheriff said grimly. "That gun killed two peace officers, so perhaps you know why I'd like for you to keep it."

"I'll keep it," King promised, and standing up, he strapped the heavy belt around his lean waist.

"I'll tell the folks in Stanhope you'll be along in a few days," the sheriff promised heartily. "Take care of yourself, Centaur King."

"I will, and *adios*," King answered with a smile, as his right hand touched the outlaw gun.

Pegasus watched the posse ride away with their grim burdens. Then he looked Centaur King over with a new look in his eyes.

"I like that better," he said judicially. "Makes you look fully dressed, if you know what I mean."

"Makes me feel different too," King admitted. "I keep expecting some bandit to pop up out of the brush and tell me to go for my hardware. I'll wear it when we are travelling, but not when we are doing our work."

Pegasus nodded and sliced bacon for the skillet.

He called it "side-meat," and he produced a can filled with eggs, each one separately wrapped in newspaper. As he unwrapped a brown egg, the boy leaned forward to stare at a picture printed on the newspaper.

"Hey, Centaur," he called excitedly. "Take a look at this!"

King took the paper and scanned the picture. Then he read the name in the caption and whistled softly.

"Gent by the name of Colt Johnson," he said slowly. "Wanted for robbery and murder, and he's a brother to Al Johnson."

"Said to be somewhere in Texas," Pegasus added. "He's a tough-looking hombre, Centaur!"

Centaur King made no reply, but again his fingers touched the handles of the outlaw gun. As though he could read the older man's thoughts, Peg Bronte spoke slowly.

"Colt Johnson will be gunning for you when he hears the news," the boy said emphatically. "He won't take no rest until he settles up for his brother!"

"Not much danger, with the law looking for him," King answered with a careless shrug, but his tone was not convincing.

"But we'll keep our eyes skimmed from now on," Peg said quietly. "I wish I had a hog-leg to wear."

"You leave firearms alone," King said sharply,

148

and then he smiled at the boy. "You kinda lose something when you carry a gun," he explained. "Something a horse can sense the minute he sees you, or gets your scent."

"Mebbe you're right, Centaur," the boy agreed humbly. "If I come up on Gold 'Un, I want him to love me, and I want him to come back!"

There was no hint of tears in Peg Bronte's brown eyes as he spoke earnestly. That was passed now, and a part of his boyhood. He seemed to have changed in some intangible manner, and now there was more of maturity to him.

"Supper is ready," he said with a smile, and the two ate their simple meal in silence.

Twilight closed in, and the night insects began to hum their nocturnal chorus. The three horses were picketed, and they made a restful, comforting sound as they grazed on the lush grass by the flowing creek.

"Tell me about the Prince of Wales," Pegasus requested. "Did he sure enough give you that pair of pistols?"

"Sure enough," King answered with a chuckle. "I went grouse shooting with him in Scotland, and he wasn't much different from you and me. He liked good horses, and good music. How about playing that old guitar some, Peg?"

Peg went to the wagon and returned with a battered guitar. He slipped a rawhide thong behind his neck, tuned the old instrument, and gently caressed the gut strings. Then he began to play softly as he sang in a boyish voice which had not full changed.

Songs of the Border country, and of the cow-trails, and then of the southland of his birth. After a while he laid the guitar aside and stared at King across the fire.

"You reckon we-uns will ever go back to Dixie?" he asked slowly.

"We'll go one day," King answered, but his tone lacked sincerity.

"I see what you mean," Pegasus murmured. "We'll go one day, and come back the next. They don't have many wild hosses down home."

"That's right," King agreed. "You better sleep in the wagon to-night, Peg."

"Colt Johnson won't find out about his brother for a while," Pegasus answered quickly. "Not until he reads about it in the papers."

"I didn't say anything about Colt Johnson," King protested.

"But you was thinking about him," the boy insisted. "I could see it in your face, and the way you rubbed the grips of that outlaw gun."

"If it shows on me that much, I'll leave off the pistol," King answered crossly.

"I didn't mean to be smart, Suh," Peg said with quick contriteness. "Please wear the gun at least while we are on the road," the boy pleaded.

"That's the way it is now," King said with

a sigh. "Let's turn in so's we can get an early start in the morning. We will pass this side of Lanthrope, and head right down to that pasture land in the valley. Should get there before dark."

"You don't want to go back to Lanthrope," Pegasus accused. "Suits me fine that away too."

Centaur King made no answer. Peg Bronte was maturing perhaps a little too rapidly. King complained to himself that the boy was getting so he could read a man's mind, and with the honesty of unspoiled youth, Peg Bronte was direct in all his ways.

"Centaur, you reckon we'll ever find Gold 'Un?" the boy asked wistfully. "You know more about hosses than any man I ever heard tell of."

"We'll find Golden," King answered positively. "If he's taken to the hills, we will have to locate him first, find the water-holes, and figure a way to snare him. Then again, he might get over being spooked and come back to find Major Domo. Those two got along uncommonly well, but there's something else again."

"Yeah, I know," Pegasus anticipated King again. "But I didn't have Gold 'Un long enough for him to love me that much."

"I believe you did," Centaur King disagreed. "I remember that first time you rode him."

"He dumped me," Pegasus said sadly.

"But you crawled him again," King pointed out. "He could have thrown you again, but he didn't.

You ever stop to reason out why he let you ride him?"

Pegasus pouted with resentment. "I thought I was the boss," he said sulkily.

"That's right," King agreed. "Every horse is looking for a master, the one person it can love and trust. When the horse finds that one person, it takes second place, and makes the master first. That's what Golden did with you, and he did it because he loved you!"

"You reckon, Centaur?" Pegasus asked in a whisper, and his brown eyes were wide with wonder.

"I'm sure of it," King said emphatically. "Now that does not mean that Golden will be an outlaw and hate everyone else. It does mean that he will leave anyone else and come to you, if you say the word."

"Thanks, pard," Pegasus murmured gratefully. "I feel better down inside now, like I was sure we would find Gold 'Un, or he will find us."

Centaur King nodded, and Pegasus climbed into the wagon. The boy undressed and slipped under his blankets, but King loitered by the fire. He sat down on an upturned bucket staring into the glowing embers. Once he glanced back over his shoulder and smiled in the fire-glow. He told himself he was getting spooks, with Pegasus reading his thoughts, but now the boy was sleeping.

To-morrow they would be back near Lanthrope, and Carol Tinsley. King stared into the coals, and he admitted to himself that Carol attracted him more than any girl he had ever met. She attracted and repelled him at the same time, and he tried to think out the reason.

He pondered about her words, the time she had told him she did not like the dominant side of his nature. He had retorted that he disliked possessiveness, and Centaur King knew that he would always have to feel free, or be miserably unhappy.

"There must be a middle course," King murmured softly, and then he shrugged and climbed into the wagon. Usually he fell asleep at once, but now he lay staring into the darkness. He felt a vague uneasiness for which he could find no reason.

The death of Al Johnson did not weigh upon his conscience; it was either kill or be killed, and self-preservation was the first law of life. He assured himself that he would find El Caballo Oro, and then his thoughts reverted again to Carol Tinsley.

"Ships that pass in the night" the girl had quoted, and now King admitted that he was again planning to avoid the girl who was so much in his thoughts. He remembered the firm roundness of her shoulder as she had leaned against him while Pegasus was making his first ride on the

153

golden stallion. He recalled the bold sure strokes of her pencil when she had sketched Pegasus and El Caballo Oro, and Centaur King stirred restlessly.

He reached out a hand and touched the holstered pistol hanging at the head of his bunk. He sobered at the thought that he was embarking on a new way of life. In a land where most men carried a six-shooter as part of their regular equipment, he had enjoyed a singular immunity. He had never worn a holstered pistol because it interfered with the nature of his work.

"I'll wear his brother's pistol until Colt Johnson finds me," Centaur King muttered.

King smiled in the darkness and closed his eyes. Soon he was breathing deeply in a sound sleep. Not until then did Pegasus Bronte sigh with a measure of content. He had heard King's whispered promise to keep himself dressed . . . like a man.

# CHAPTER ELEVEN
## ONE LOVE

Thunderheads were roaring above the low Sandia Mountains to arouse Centaur King and Pegasus from slumber. A leaden dawn gave promise of rain, and the three picketed horses were nervous. King told the boy to hurry breakfast while he harnessed the restive team, and they hurried through the meal without conversation.

Texas rains in mid-summer usually meant flash-floods where all the dry water-ways ran banks full to make travel difficult. There were no bridges across the shallow creeks, which meant that crossing would be impossible through the fords if much rain should fall.

Centaur King took the driver's seat and kicked off the stout brake. Then they were rolling eastward toward Lanthrope, but in a somewhat different fashion than the first time they had visited the town. Now Centaur King was fully dressed, and the black-butted gun seemed a part of his attire.

Pegasus Bronte seemed on edge, and his narrowed eyes watched the brush-fringe which bordered the road. He breathed easier when they were again on higher ground and out of the brakes where there was too much cover to hide an ambusher.

King remained silent as he handled the trotting team of bays but he knew that Pegasus was thinking about Colt Johnson. Both relaxed when they came to an open prairie, and the boy jumped when the thunderheads knocked together with a dull grinding roar. A moment later the rain was pelting down in torrents, and Pegasus handed King a slicker as the older man stopped the teams for a blow.

"There's going to be dirty weather," King said quietly. "We will be hub-deep in mud if this keeps up an hour."

"She's a portent, Centaur," the boy said gravely. "A good storm will mebbe so clear up the air."

King nodded as he glanced sideways at the sober-faced boy. Evidently Pegasus had not slept well, and he was as jumpy as the team of bays which required careful handling every time the lightning flashed across the low hills.

Now the dirt road was boggy, and the iron-shod wheels slipped on the turns. But Centaur King was a master reinsman, and he knew just how much to use the brakes to help the hard-working horses.

"Reminds me some of that bayou country down Louisiana way," Pegasus remarked.

Centaur nodded as he scanned the prairie land ahead. Here and there ancient buffalo wallows were filled with rain water, and the gramma grass was showing green where the rain had scoured away the thick coatings of dust.

Progress was slow, and the conversation was desultory. The two spoke only about the roads and the weather, and remarked about the cattle they could see grazing on the unfenced range.

A long stop was made at noon to rest the weary horses, and after feeding them a measure of grain, Pegasus climbed into the wagon and made cold meat sandwiches. King climbed in after going over the wagon gear, and for a moment he stared at the lumps of gumbo mud that clung to their boots.

"This shere won't last long," Pegasus said, and he tried to make his voice cheerful. "I'll clean this up in a jiffy after it stops raining and dries out a bit."

"It's going to be slide and pull the rest of the way," King warned. "I've been thinking, Peg. We'll outspan on that high little knoll near the cottonwoods just above the creek, when we reach that pasture land."

"Good thing we put in that gate." The boy held up his end of the talk. "You reckon we can get the wagon up on that knoll?"

Centaur King nodded. He knew the pulling power of his team of matched bays, and the Conestoga wagon had been built to his order. The harness was the best that money could buy, and in perfect condition. Pegasus always saw to that, and he would be busy for days cleaning and oiling up the gear, after the storm had passed to the north.

At last they were on the move again, and the roads were even worse when they turned southeast and headed down into the valley. It was late afternoon when they stopped to rest the team after a hard pull through a soupy mud hole. King pointed to a bosque of scrub-oak to the right, and then he handed the heavy reins to Pegasus.

"The team will need some help from here on," King said quietly. "I'll throw that old stock saddle on Major Domo, and tie on to the wagon tongue. We're almost home, Peg!"

"Yeah," the boy answered with a sigh. "We can camp on our own land for a change."

King climbed from the wagon and rubbed the black stallion down with a dry rag. The big horse rumbled in his throat, and whickered softly when King brought out the heavy stock saddle. Major Domo knew there was work to do, and he was eager to get about it.

King told Pegasus that he would ride ahead and open the gate, and he mounted the stallion and rode away. It was about a quarter of a mile from the wagon to the gate, and King stared at the top rail of the heavy gate as he rode alongside. There were fresh scars on the seasoned wood, and then King noticed some deep hoof-prints where a rider had passed since the rains had let up.

His eyes narrowed as he sat saddle to study the sign. Then he swung down and opened the gate, and he removed the yellow slicker and tied it to the cantle of his saddle. His right hand dropped down and touched the heavy gun in his holster, after which King shrugged irritably.

He told himself that he was getting jumpy as he again mounted Major Domo. Pegasus had started the team, and was halfway to the new land. He stopped the team and set his brake like an old-timer, and Centaur King uncoiled his lariat and made fast the wagon tongue.

"You see anything yonder, Centaur?" Pegasus asked eagerly.

"I say a lot of tracks where Jim Stacey's men had run that hoss-band in," King replied. "And it looked to me like a hoss-backer had gone through the gate since the last storm let up, but I couldn't be sure. Like as not it was one of Stacey's riders getting back to town."

"Like as not," Pegasus agreed, but King saw that the boy had placed the shotgun on the wagonseat close to his hand.

"Keep the team pulling when we go through the gate," he told the boy. "Keep a light foot on the brake to stop the wagon from side-slipping on that little rise. Let's go!"

Major Domo fiddle-footed out in front of the team, but King held him steady. The bays shouldered into the collars, and the wagon started rolling. Peg Bronte handled the lines expertly, and when they came to the gate, King straightened the stallion out and tightened the catch-rope.

Peg Bronte was too busy to notice any of the signs as they lumbered sluggishly through the mud and started up the rise toward the cottonwood knoll. The stout bays were hock-deep in mud, but pulling together handsomely. The wagon lurched and hesitated, and Centaur King spoke quietly to Major Domo.

"Belly down, boy. Show that team what you can do!"

The black stallion did not lurch against the rope. He stepped ahead cautiously until the rope grew taut. Then Major Domo grunted and added his weight to the task. The heavy wagon started rolling smoothly up the slippery grade, with the three horses digging in to lighten the common task.

Major Domo reached the knoll and slacked off the rope. The team of bays came over with the load, and Peg Bronte set his brakes and jumped to the ground. The shotgun was in his hands as he hit the boggy grass, but after searching the grazing land intently, he replaced the weapon on the wagon-seat and unfastened his tugs.

"We've got to rub the hosses down good and give 'em a double measure of grain," Peg said to King. "They earned it, and a better team I've never tooled in all my life!"

Centaur King nodded, and he did not smile. Peg Bronte was growing up, and he did a man's work. He dismounted from the stallion and tied Major Domo to a rear wheel. Then they removed the heavy harness and hung it on pegs at the rear of the wagon.

The skies had cleared, and twilight was closing in when the two had finished their chores. Centaur King turned to Peg Bronte with a little smile curling his lips. And in the horse tamer's eyes was a light of deep understanding.

"Major Domo will carry double, Peg," he said slowly. "You and me are riding down to the water-hole near the creek to see what we can see."

"Centaur!" the boy exclaimed eagerly. "Do you reckon . . . ? You think mebbe Gold 'Un . . . ?"

"Let's not build our hopes too high, Peg," King cautioned. "Didn't want to get you upset with the work to do, but I read some sign when I rode on ahead here to open the gate. Looked to me like a lone hoss had topped that gate, but I could be wrong."

"Dogies!" Peg whispered. "Let's get on down there, Centaur. I want to see that El Caballo Oro so bad I can taste it!"

King mounted Major Domo and kicked the left stirrup loose for Peg. The boy climbed up behind the cantle, and Major Domo shook himself to balance the double weight. Then they were riding down the gentle slope through the cottonwoods, and they followed the swollen creek up toward the far south end of the pasture which was fenced with heavy stake-and-rider poles.

Alders and willows fringed the creek banks where the lush grass grew high. Centaur King reached down suddenly when the stallion pricked his ears forward. King grabbed Major Domo's nose to prevent the stallion from whinnying, and he told Pegasus to slide down and slip a latigo-string over the stallion's nose.

"We'll go on foot from here," King whispered, as he dismounted. "The hoss-band is up ahead; and we'll see what we will see."

Pegasus Bronte was trembling with eagerness as the two made their way among the willows. Now it was almost dark, and Centaur King loosened the heavy six-shooter in his holster. They made scarcely any sound as they crept forward, and Peg Bronte sucked in his breath when King held out a hand for a halt.

Up through the trees they could see a deep hole where the bending creek had cut a back-wash. The horse-band was standing at the far side, watching something with ears pricked forward.

"It's a man!" Peg Bronte whispered.

"Quiet!" King muttered sternly. "It's a woman!"

"Carol Tinsley!" he heard the boy whisper

angrily. "Look, Centaur. There's Gold 'Un!"

"Quiet!" King hissed, and he hunkered down on his boot-heels to watch.

Carol Tinsley was facing a clump of willows with her left hand outstretched. Her boots and divided leather skirt were muddy, and the girl was crooning softly. A dozen paces away the golden stallion was facing her with his head high, and nostrils flaring.

"Come, Golden!" they heard the girl plead softly. "Come here, I say!"

"She's stealing our stuff!" Pegasus whispered hotly. "I got to go, Centaur!"

"Wait!" King ordered sternly. "This is another test, Peg. We will see how much Gold 'Un loves you!"

The golden stallion took a step forward and stopped. Carol Tinsley spoke again, and now her voice was commanding.

"Come here, Golden! Come here, I say!"

El Caballo Oro tossed his head and then came forward. He stopped near the motionless girl, stretched out his neck, and sniffed at her extended hand. Carol watched for a long moment, and then she took a little step and patted the big horse on the neck.

Gold 'Un stood and submitted to the caresses. Centaur King turned to Pegasus, and the boy was clenching his teeth.

"A good horse chooses one master," King said

in a whisper. "Give that whistle you use to call Golden!"

Peg Bronte changed then. He gasped and swayed a trifle. Then his eyes lighted up with a great love as he watched the golden stallion. At last he took a deep breath, and a high treble whistle keened from his lips.

The golden stallion threw up his head and whinnied eagerly. Pegasus whistled his double call again, and the stallion leaped into a gallop from a standing start. Then he was coming through the willows at a dead run, straight to the spot where Pegasus waited in a little clearing.

Centaur King had stepped back, and he watched the big horse slide to a stop when he saw Peg Bronte. Pegasus whistled softly, and the stallion leaped at him and nuzzled the boy's shoulder. Peg held on to keep from being rubbed down, and his arms went around the great arched neck.

"Gold 'Un," he sobbed. "I was a-breakin' my heart over losin' you, Gold 'Un. Don't you ever high-tail and leave me no more, you slab-sided, wall-eyed knock-kneed old jughead!"

The golden stallion crowded up close to the boy, nuzzling Pegasus with little whickers of delight. Peg Bronte stroked the beautiful animal, and then he reached for the little looped thong which still dangled from the halter. He turned swiftly when a voice spoke behind and off to the side.

"Pegasus! I didn't know you were back!"

"Thanks for letting my hoss in the paster," Pegasus said in a low voice.

"But I didn't let him in," the girl answered. "I rode over to see if the horse-band was all right, and I saw Golden jump over the gate and gallop down here to the creek. He left me and came to you," she added reproachfully.

"That's what ever," Peg agreed. "A good horse always looks about for one master, and then he gives that one all his love!"

"But he came to me," Carol said quickly, and her tone was resentful. "It took me two hours to coax him up to my hand, and then you spoiled everything when you whistled!"

"Yes'm," the boy agreed. "That there was the test, Miss Carol. It would have made a big difference if Gold 'Un hadn't come when I called!"

"How did he get away?" the girl asked.

"Me and Centaur was held up by Road Agents," Peg answered importantly. "They tried to steal Gold 'Un, but he broke loose and high-tailed it back toward Lanthrope. Centaur killed one of those hombres, and Major Domo broke the other outlaw's neck!"

"You say Centaur King killed a man?" the girl asked in a horrified whisper.

Centaur King had gone back for Major Domo, and he rode up in time to hear the girl's question.

He heard Pegasus answer with a note of pride in his drawling voice.

"Shot him deader than four o'clock!" Peg Bronte boasted.

King rode into the clearing and raised his rain-soaked Stetson. "Howdy, Miss Carol," he said softly. "It was mighty neighbourly of you to ride over and look after our stock."

"I'm so glad to see you again, Centaur!" the girl answered with a little lilt in her voice, and then she stepped back with an expression of repugnance mirrored in her rounded eyes. "You are carrying a gun!" she gasped.

"Yes, Carol," King answered quietly. "I was going to ride over to see your brother Crag. Tell him there is a killer loose in these parts; a man by the name of Colt Johnson!"

"And you killed a man," the girl murmured. "Was it . . . necessary?"

"I'll tell a man!" Peg Bronte interrupted. "He was shooting at Centaur, but he only got one slug away when Centaur fined his sights and knocked that buscadero outen his saddle!"

"It was self-defence, Carol," King explained with a note of strain in his deep voice. "This man was an outlaw by the name of Al Johnson, and he was brother to Colt Johnson. It was Al Johnson who tried to steal El Caballo Oro, and he shot several times at the golden stallion when the horse broke away."

"I'll tell Crag," the girl murmured. "It is almost dark, and I must be getting back to the ranch."

"I'll ride with you," King offered eagerly.

"Please," the girl protested. "I will be perfectly safe, and you would not know the way back!"

Centaur King reined his horse back with a stricken look in his brown eyes. Then he nodded his head and replaced his soggy Stetson.

"As you will," he murmured. "Perhaps you'd like Pegasus to ride over with you."

"I've got to look after Gold 'Un," the boy interrupted rudely. "He loves me the best, and I've got to look after him!"

"Yes, Peg, he loves you the best," Carol Tinsley agreed softly. "Please be very good to him."

"Yes'm," Peg answered in a shamed voice. "You meant Gold 'Un, didn't you?" he asked quickly, and watched the girl's face.

"Good-bye now, and perhaps I'll see you all to-morrow," Carol said hastily, and turning abruptly, she ran down the trail to a nest of scrub-oak where she had left her horse.

"Pegasus!" Centaur King said sternly, and he waited for the boy to face him. "What did you mean by that impertinent question?" King demanded.

"Gee, Centaur, I'm sorry if I said the wrong thing," Pegasus answered contritely. "I kinda got all mixed up there, on account of Miss Carol was looking at you when she was talking to me!"

"You embarrassed the lady," King accused softly, but his voice was very gentle. "Sometimes you only think what you think, Peg," he continued. "You're almost man-size now, and you don't blurt out everything you might be thinking, especially to a lady!"

"But Miss Carol was thinking out loud," Peg murmured miserably. "I'm sorry, Centaur," he whispered. "I didn't mean any impudence, cross my heart and spit!"

He illustrated his earnestness by crossing his heart and spitting behind his cupped hand. King smiled and slowly mounted Major Domo.

"Climb that wall-eyed knothead, and let's ride back to the wagon," he said quietly.

"Gold 'Un ain't no knothead," Peg defended loyally.

"I heard you calling him out of his name," King retorted.

"That there was different," Peg answered. "That was love-talk, and Gold 'Un knew it!"

"Sure, I know," King answered with a chuckle. "But let's ride to the wagon and clean up some. Then we will go into town for supper, and we just might see the marshal."

"You won't lay your gun aside, Centaur, will you?" the boy asked anxiously.

Centaur King's jaw tightened. "That I won't!" he answered crisply. "Not while Colt Johnson is on the prowl!"

Pegasus smiled happily and mounted the golden stallion with a little jump. Then he rode bareback through the dusky gloom, and all the worry was gone from his sensitive face as he stroked the arching neck beneath his hand.

"He loves me the best," he murmured softly, and the golden stallion whickered with quiet content.

# CHAPTER TWELVE
## BUSH-WHACKER

Centaur King was standing by the big wagon staring into the darkness beyond the gate in the stake-and-rider fence when Peg Bronte rode up on Golden. King whirled suddenly with a mixture of anxiety and determination showing on his sensitive features.

"Saddle up Golden and close the gate after you, Peg!" the horse tamer said tensely. "I shouldn't have left Miss Carol ride on alone after dark, and I'm going ahead to see that she comes to no harm!"

He leaped to the saddle and was gone on Major Domo before the boy could offer a protest, and Peg Bronte wasted no time in obeying orders. He leaped inside the wagon and brought out his light saddle, brushed the stallion down hurriedly, and cinched the hull in place. He changed the halter for a hackamore bridle, and the stallion whinnied with eagerness to take after his trail-mate.

Pegasus stopped to close the gate and then roared up the muddy road after King. Golden was a natural mudder, and the big horse was sure-footed. A sense of power flooded through the boy as he felt the drive of those powerful flanks beneath him, but he could see nothing ahead in the darkness except a short strip of the road.

Centaur King was thinking of Carol Tinsley as he sat a deep saddle and allowed Major Domo to pick his own way. The big black ran with head slightly down, avoiding the deeper puddles by instinct. They were perhaps ten minutes on the road to Lanthrope when Major Domo shied to the right and then whinnied a call.

King saw a darker blotch up ahead and called an inquiry. "Is that you, Miss Carol?"

"Centaur!" came the answer. "I'm so glad you came!"

King rode closer and spoke cheerily. "I didn't stop to clean up, and I'm sorry I didn't come along with you in the first place."

He felt a small hand on his left arm, and the warmth of the girl's touch started the horse tamer's blood to racing. His soggy Stetson was hand-shaped to fit his face, and he turned to Carol Tinsley with a little smile. Then she realized that she could not see his face in the darkness, because he could not see hers.

"I'm sorry I was rude, Centaur," she said in a low voice. "Of course you will have to go armed after what has happened. Crag has always carried a six-shooter, and I never thought anything about it, but it seemed so different with you."

"Different?" King repeated. "Yes," he admitted readily. "A gun really does not fit in with my profession, Miss Carol. It arouses something within a man which an animal can recognize at once."

"And a woman," Carol added. "I sensed the difference in you the moment I saw you wearing that pistol."

"I had no choice," King explained. "The sheriff gave me the gun and asked me to wear it."

"I understand now," the girl said quietly. "I heard Crag talking about those three outlaws, and they usually travelled together."

"Colt Johnson is a lone wolf now," King answered. "And more dangerous than before."

"He escaped from prison," Carol said, and her voice betrayed a deep agitation. "It was Crag who arrested Colt Johnson and sent him to prison," she added with a shudder.

"I should have rode into Lanthrope and warned Crag," King censored himself.

"But you didn't know," the girl made excuse. "Colt Johnson swore that he'd kill Crag if it took the rest of his life!"

"We will warn him right away," King said soothingly. "Pegasus is following me on Golden, and we are going to have supper in town. Will you join us, Miss Carol?"

"I'm too dirty after riding all afternoon," the girl made her excuse. "You will ask me another time?"

Before King could answer, a six-shooter flamed

through the darkness just ahead. They could see the board sidewalks which marked the beginning of town, and Centaur King touched his horse with a heel. Then he was racing toward a man who was lying on the boardwalk, and he made a running dismount and slid to a stop beside the wounded man.

"You hurt bad, pard?" he asked sharply.

"Centaur!" came the gasping answer. "It's Crag Tinsley, and I was bushed from the dark!"

"How bad are you hurt?" King asked, as he knelt beside the marshal.

"High in the left breast," Tinsley gasped painfully. "I took another slug in the right leg!"

"Did you see your assailant?" King asked.

"A tall thin hombre straddling a grey bronc," Tinsley gave the description slowly, and then he recognized his sister as Carol came to his side. "Carol," the wounded marshal gasped. "What are you doing down here at this time of night?"

"Riding in to warn you, but I'm too late," Carol Tinsley sobbed. "Colt Johnson broke out of prison!"

"By Dogies!" Tinsley almost shouted. "I knew there was something familiar about the set of that killer's shoulders. It was Colt Johnson!"

Centaur King was leaning over the wounded marshal, pressing a handkerchief tight against the chest wound. He jerked up suddenly as the sharp spitting bark of a light pistol roared twenty yards down the street, and then he heard the thud of racing hooves as a horseman sped away in the opposite direction. Then came a boyish shout from the dark.

"It's me, Centaur. Peg Bronte!"

Centaur King faced around and waited for Pegasus to come out of the dark. The boy was holding one of the light duelling pistols, and Carol stared at him with something of the horror depicted in her eyes she had expressed when she saw King with a pistol strapped on his right leg.

"Who did you shoot at?" King asked sternly.

"Some bush-whacker," Peg Bronte answered excitedly. "I heard shooting up this way as I raced into town, and I tied up Golden when I saw you under that light. I was coming up on foot when I see this skinny hombre sitting a grey hoss back there in the shadows, and he was lining his gun down on your back. I snapped a shot at him, but I don't think I hurt him very bad!"

"Thanks, Peg," King said quietly. "That killer was Colt Johnson, and he dry-gulched Marshal Tinsley. He don't know about me yet, but he meant to kill me because I was siding the law."

King did not scold the boy for taking one of his treasured duelling pistols. Now his concern was for the wounded marshal, but Crag Tinsley spoke first.

"You said you was siding the law?" he asked King.

"In a manner of speaking," King answered evasively.

"Centaur killed Al Johnson yesterday," Carol Tinsley interrupted. "Sheriff Clay gave Centaur the gun Johnson was wearing, and you know what that means, Crag!"

"Hold up your right hand and say 'I do,' and don't give me an argument," Tinsley said weakly. "I'm making you a deputy marshal!"

"Thanks, no," King refused quietly. "But I will do what I can to help, and now I'll take care of myself!"

"Better do it the law way," Tinsley cautioned.

"Self-defence is always permissible under the law," King said steadily. "Now we've got to get you home, and under a doctor's care."

"One side!" a gruff voice ordered brusquely, and a white-haired man pushed King aside and set a little black bag on the boardwalk. "How bad you hurt, Crag?" he asked anxiously.

"Not too bad, but losing blood," Tinsley answered. "Dr. Snyder, this is Centaur King!"

"Ah, yes, the horse tamer," the old Medico said gruffly. "Well, don't just stand there gaping like a lout. Cut the leg of the marshal's pants down the seam, and I'll apply a tourniquet. You, Button," he roared at Pegasus. "Run up to the livery barn and tell Hank White to get down here pronto with his buckboard. Git going!"

The crotchety old doctor barked orders at Carol

and King, but he went about his work with a deft knowledge which won the horse tamer's admiration. When Peg Bronte rode back with the liveryman, Doc Snyder said that his patient was ready to travel.

"Easy does it now, you bronc-stompers!" the doctor ordered. "Make a cradle lift and raise him up so. Don't stumble, you big ox!" he snarled at Hank White. "Stop blubbering, gal," he told Carol who was trying to restrain her sobs.

"Aw, shut up, you old buzzard!" Crag Tinsley growled at the old doctor.

"That's going to cost you, my star-toting *amigo*," Doc Snyder told the wounded man. "Wait until I probe for those slugs, and you'll sing a different tune!"

He turned and winked at Centaur King without smiling, and somehow King felt better. He told Carol to ride with the doctor, said he'd lead her horse and ride up with Pegasus to help undress the marshal and get him to bed.

Supper was forgotten as the two horse tamers followed the buckboard to the other end of town where Hank White stopped in front of a neat white cottage. Carol hastened inside to warn the marshal's wife, and Rose Tinsley came out to press her husband's hand.

"You'll be all right, darlin'," she whispered. "I'm so glad Mr. King is here to help!"

"In more ways than one," Tinsley murmured

weakly, and then he lost consciousness as they lifted him from the buckboard.

The two women had stripped back a low couch in the big front room, and the doctor barked orders for clean cloths and plenty of boiling water. Centaur King removed the marshal's boots, and Pegasus helped undress the wounded man. Doc Snyder turned on the boy roughly.

"Does the sight of blood make you sick?" he demanded.

"Naw," Peg Bronte barked back at him. "Centaur killed him an owl-hooter yesterday, and I never turned a hair!"

"That will do, Peg," King warned sternly.

"You say you killed a man?" Doc Snyder asked with interest. "Anyone I know?"

"It was Al Johnson, Doc," the liveryman volunteered the answer. "Him and Pete Powers stuck up King and tried to steal the two stallions. Johnson took a free shot at Centaur, but King burned that owl-hooter down with one shot!"

"Wait a minute," the doctor said, and now he appeared worried. "You killed Al Johnson, and his brother Colt tried to kill the marshal. Better hunt a hole, hoss tamer," he advised. "Colt Johnson is a dangerous hombre, and he'll ride gun-sign on you as soon as he hears the news!"

"Here's the hot water and bandages," King said carelessly, as the two women returned from the kitchen.

178

"Don't tell me my business!" the old Medico snapped.

"Don't tell me mine," King said coldly. "Do you want my help?"

"Hump!" the doctor sniffed. "I'll need it," he admitted ungraciously. "But you look alive now, and mind what I tell you. Hold this tray under that leg while I bathe it some."

"Yes, Doctor," King answered quietly.

"Hand me that probe!" the doctor barked.

"Yes, Doctor!"

"You 'Yes, Doctor' me one more time, and I'm going to do you a meanness!" the old Medico threatened. "Now hold on to your innards and don't go to fainting!"

"Okay, Doc!" King answered without smiling, and the old doctor grinned his appreciation. Then he went about his work deftly, and a moment later he laid a leaden slug on the tray.

"Not bad," he remarked. "I'll dress and bandage that piddling flesh wound, and we'll have a look up above." He turned on Peg Bronte when a suspicious sound reached his ears. "Take that button outside!" the doctor roared at Carol Tinsley who was watching from the kitchen. "This is no place for that young 'un to be sick!"

As Carol put an arm around Peg and guided him through the back door the doctor spoke softly to Centaur King.

"This might be serious, King. I want you to

keep busy with these sponges while I probe. Once I start, I can't stop, so get a grip on yourself!"

"I'm ready, Doc," King whispered softly. "Crag couldn't have a better surgeon, so let's get it done!"

"The hell you say!" the old Medico growled, but he gripped King by the hand and started to work.

Hank White gulped and tip-toed shakily from the room. Carol Tinsley came in and said she had scrubbed her hands good, and the doctor told her to close the kitchen door. "Help King with the tray and sponges," the doctor said, without looking up from his work.

Carol Tinsley came to stand beside Centaur King who was rinsing his hands in a solution the doctor had mixed. Carol also rinsed her hands, and her face was white as she stared down at the bullet hole in her brother's left breast. Centaur King found her hand and gripped it assuringly, and Carol smiled faintly to show her appreciation.

"Sponge!" the doctor barked testily. "Hold that tray steady to catch the drainage!"

"Okay, Doc," King answered in a steady voice, and he applied the surgical sponge deftly, and with a hand that did not tremble.

Carol turned away when the old doctor asked for his probes. Centaur King nodded and obeyed instantly, and then he was busy with the sponges. Carol sighed when she heard the rattle on the tray to tell that the bullet had been removed, but the two men were too busy to notice.

"Just missed the lung," the doctor told King. "Don't know what in Tophet I'd have done without you, you hoss tamer!"

"A man does what comes to his hand," King answered with a smile, but Carol Tinsley noticed that he now seemed weary.

"Hold that compress while I start this bandage," the doctor barked. "Easy now," he complained irritably. "That's the first time I saw you shake to-night. You going sissy on me at this stage of the game?"

"Yeah, Doc," King answered honestly. "I'm so hungry I could sleep for a week. We had a skimpy breakfast, a sandwich for dinner, and no supper!"

"Well, why didn't you say so?" the doctor demanded irritably. "You, Carol!" he shouted at the girl. "Tell Rose that Crag will be as good as new, and you throw some hot vittles together for these hoss tamers. What in tarnation do you think they are, iron men?"

"Yes, Doctor," Carol answered meekly, and the old Medico glared at her as he paused from his bandaging. "Okay, Doc," the girl corrected herself, and Doc Snyder beamed as he winked at King.

"Mighty fine little filly, that Carol gal," he remarked confidentially. "I brought her into this world, and I ought to know!"

181

"I'm not arguing with you, Doc," King said meekly.

"See that you don't," Doc Snyder warned. "Sooner or later all these tough cases have to call on me, and that's when I get back a bit of my own!"

"Okay, Doc," King agreed. "You mind if I wash up now and look after my pard?"

"You tell the button I'm sorry, and that I didn't know he was weak from hunger," the doctor whispered. "Fine boy, that Peg Bronte. I said the same thing when he tamed that big golden stud!"

"I'll tell him, Doc," King promised, and went in search of Peg Bronte.

Carol stopped him and told him to wash at a basin in the sink. She leaned close to King and told him in a whisper how much his help had meant to her. Rose Tinsley added her thanks, and told King he would find Pegasus in the next room.

Carol placed a finger on her lips in warning, and led King to the door. It was open a crack, and Centaur King looked through the crack. He smiled when he saw Peg Bronte sitting in a big rocker with little Madeline wrapped in a blanket, held tightly in his arms. Peg's cheek rested on the little girl's curly blonde head, and they were both sleeping soundly.

"He's a darling," Carol whispered. "He asked

Rose if he could see Sugar Foots, and Rose didn't even smile. She led Peg in here, and Madeline was awake. She was in his arms before Peg knew what was happening, and she fussed with him until he kissed her."

Centaur King looked at the sleeping pair with a queer little tightening of the throat. He turned slowly to look at Carol, and she swayed toward him with her eyes brimming with unshed tears. Then Centaur King's arms were around her, and he patted her shoulder gently as she gave way to her tears.

King didn't say anything; there didn't seem to be any need for words. So much had happened since morning when the storm had threatened to bar their return to Lanthrope. Carol had seemed so far away and inaccessible, and now she was in his arms.

Carol dried her tears and gently released herself. She smiled at King and told him that supper would soon be ready, and asked him to awaken Pegasus. Then she returned to the kitchen, and Centaur King stood like a man in a dream for a long moment.

Then he drew a deep breath and softly opened the door. Peg Bronte opened his eyes instantly and gasped.

"Dadburn me, Centaur," he made his excuses hurriedly. "I must have dozed off there for a minute, me and Sugar Foots. Coming right up!"

"Hold me, Peggie," the little girl wailed, as she aroused sleepily.

"Peg!" the boy corrected. "Say it, before I drop you on the floor."

"Don't go away, Peg!" Madeline pleaded.

"Peg and I are going to have supper now," Centaur King explained to the little girl. "You better cuddle down in bed, and Peg will see you later!"

"Kiss me, Peg," Madeline insisted.

"Aw, Sugar, quit it!" Pegasus growled, but he bent his head and kissed the child. Then he carried her to her little bed and tucked her in, and Rose Tinsley smiled at him and told him to be seated at the table across from Centaur King.

"I want to thank you both," she said quietly. "We won't ever forget what you did for us to-night!"

# CHAPTER THIRTEEN
## THE MEDDLER

Doc Snyder was scrubbing at the kitchen sink. His snowy-white hair made a halo above the saturnine cast of his wrinkled features. The long nose curved slightly to meet puckered lips, and bushy brows shadowed a pair of keen blue eyes which saw everything, and understood most of what they saw.

The old Medico dried his hands on a towel Carol handed him, came over and took a seat at the table near Centaur King, and stared thoughtfully at the horse tamer's glowing eyes. Doc Snyder nodded and took a hand in a game in which he had bought no chips.

"That tonic was good for what ailed you, King," he said dogmatically. "Man was not meant to live alone, nor woman either, for that matter!"

Centaur King rested both hands on the table and stopped eating. He cocked his head to one side as though to listen, and he did not look at the old doctor. Instead, he met Carol Tinsley's eyes, and the girl's face flushed rosily.

"Tonic?" King asked quietly, but two spots of colour leaped to his high cheek-bones. "Perhaps I do not understand what you mean, Doc."

"Sassafras and Iodefoam!" Doc Snyder snorted. "You are a strong self-contained man, with many good points, and just as many faults!"

Centaur King raised his eyes and stared at the old doctor with the trace of a smile on his full lips. Pegasus was listening intently without interrupting, but the boy's face showed a definite resentment.

"You should be a hoss-trader, Doc," King said slowly. "You can read off a critter's points and ear-markings at a glance."

"After careful study and under fire," Doc Snyder corrected sharply. "Not many men could do what you did to-night, and not many men have the sureness of touch you possess in those hands of yours. Trouble with you is, your mind has been too well disciplined!"

"If I ever get shot, I'll come to you for treatment," King replied coldly. "I hardly think that this is the time or place to give me a mental examination!"

"Treacle and brimstone!" Doc Snyder snorted. "You helped me when I needed help badly, and now I mean to help you. You'd make a valuable and useful citizen if you would settle down somewhere and stop this traipsing around all over creation. What you need is a loyal and devoted wife, and a couple of little Princes of your own!"

"Wouldn't you settle for a Prince and a Princess?" King asked lightly. "And wouldn't I need a castle to complete your fairy tale?"

"Yeah, that's right," the doctor agreed, not in the least abashed. "But you want to remember that a man's home is his castle, and that home is where the heart is!"

"How long do you think Crag will be laid up?" King changed the subject abruptly.

"Three weeks, mebbe a month," the doctor answered professionally. He packed an old briar pipe with tobacco and lighted the fragrant weed. Then he slowly sipped a cup of coffee with a little smile puckering his thin lips.

"I've seen 'em come and go, the drifters and the boomers," he stated crisply. "They don't amount to much until they stop drifting and booming, and settle down on their own land."

"But the marshal won't be crippled any," King said confidently, and with a little smile of gratitude. "Thanks to your efforts in the profession for which you were trained, Doc Snyder!"

The old Medico hooted and waved his pipe. "None are so blind as those who will not see!" he quoted wrathfully. "So it's none of my blasted business. I'm just an old busy-body who goes around sticking his long nose in other people's business!"

"Call yourself names, Doc," King agreed with

a slow and irritating smile. "Of course you left instructions for Mrs. Tinsley?"

"I give up!" Doc Snyder declared, with an air of injured innocence, as he knocked the ash from his pipe and rose to his feet. "But I'm sticking my nose in your business just one more time, young feller me lad," he said sternly. "Watch your back, and keep your hand right close to that gun on your odd leg!"

"That's a promise, Doc," King answered quietly, and now the smile had fled from his face to leave it set and hard.

There was silence in the kitchen after Hank White had driven away with the doctor. Rose Tinsley tried to make conversation, and then she went in to sit beside the wounded marshal. Madeline called for Pegasus who excused himself and went in to talk to the child. Carol was left with Centaur King who was slowly sipping a cup of hot coffee.

"He's really an old dear, Centaur," the girl made conversation.

"And he has right good judgment," King agreed, to surprise the girl. "He goes around planting seeds, hoping that a few of them will fall on fertile soil."

"You will be careful, Centaur?" Carol pleaded, and there was a trace of fear in her eyes. "With Colt Johnson loose and living for nothing except revenge?"

Centaur King's hand dropped down and his fingers touched the handles of the heavy six-shooter in his holster. "I'll be careful," he assured the girl. "I've been thinking, Carol," he continued thoughtfully. "Thinking how all things seem to add up and fit together."

"I don't believe I understand," Carol answered hesitantly.

"Me changing my mind about going into Stanhope and coming back to hunt for Golden," King explained. "Then we cut away from Lanthrope and went down to the pasture in the valley. We found you there, and we found Golden. Then I decided to come to town for supper, and to overtake you. Pegasus had to saddle his horse, and he trailed along behind. We got there in time to scare Colt Johnson away, and Pegasus got there just in time to save my life. Doc Snyder needed a bit of help, and everything worked out as though it had been planned."

"There are no accidents in Destiny," Carol quoted. "I read that line somewhere, and I have never forgotten it."

"You are a beautiful girl," Centaur King said in his slow drawl. "You have talent and charm, and a deep sense of responsibility."

"Thank you," Carol murmured, and she began to clear away the dishes.

Centaur King flushed as he thought of his own evaluation of Doc Snyder, who went about sowing seeds which sometimes fell upon fertile soil. Then an expression of resolve squared the horse tamer's jaw as he rose to his feet. Carol was busy at the sink, and Centaur King stepped behind her and circled the startled girl with his strong arms. He bent her head back and kissed her full on the lips, and his arms tightened when she struggled to escape.

"I love you, Carol," he murmured with his lips close to her ear. "I've been very restless since I left Lanthrope and you."

Carol lifted her hands from the dish pan and dried them on her apron. For a long moment she remained passive, and strangely silent. Then she slowly turned, and King loosened his arms long enough to allow her to face him. For another long moment Carol studied his darkly handsome face.

"Perhaps I love you too, Centaur," she said wistfully. "I'm not sure, because of the resentment you sometimes arouse in me, but I've been restless ever since I met you."

"Time will adjust our differences," King murmured. "We have much in common."

"And many views for which we do not find a solution," Carol reminded.

Centaur King's strong fingers slipped up and closed upon the girl's rounded shoulders. His head lowered a trifle to meet her troubled eyes, and Carol met his gaze without wavering.

190

"But you do love me," King said softly. "Kiss me, Carol!"

"No!"

Centaur King smiled, and the girl felt his arms tremble slightly. Then she felt the magnetic vibration of his strong fingers, and she swayed closer to him.

"Kiss me, I say!" Centaur King whispered.

Carol Tinsley stiffened and stepped back so swiftly that she was out of his arms before King divined her intention. She raised her head proudly, and her eyes sparkled with resentment as she faced him with more than a suggestion of anger in her throaty voice.

"I won't, horse tamer!" she flung at him defiantly. "And don't you dare use that commanding tone to me!"

Centaur King stared with his lips slightly parted. A stubborn expression flashed in his dark eyes as he faced the girl who had aroused within him the first fires of a virgin love. He had never felt the same toward another woman; had never spoken of love.

"Come to me, Carol," he said gently, and then his voice grew stronger. "Come here, I say!"

Carol Tinsley started forward and then stopped. Her lips pouted momentarily, and then stiffened into a straight line of resistance.

"I won't!" she said coldly. "You might have the

gift with wild horses, but I refuse to be classified under that category!"

Centaur King listened and then his shoulders began to droop. A flush of colour tinted his cheeks as he turned away with a look of startled shame changing the somewhat arrogant expression of his eyes.

"I am sorry, Carol," he murmured just above his breath. "I will never try to dominate you again. Can you forgive me?"

Carol Tinsley watched the transformation, and she felt a little tug of dismay at her heart. Gone was the masterful confidence she had admired so many times, and she was not sure that she liked the change. Now she wanted to take him in her arms as a mother would comfort a child who has been severely punished.

She took a step forward, and the door to Madeline's bedroom opened slowly. Pegasus Bronte came into the kitchen with his dinky hat in one hand, and he went directly to King and touched the silent man gently on the arm.

"We forgot about the horses, Centaur," the boy reminded hurriedly. "If Golden should take off again, he might not come back!"

Centaur King turned and regained his composure as his mind snapped back to realities.

"That's right, Peg," he agreed heartily, and with a certain degree of relief. "And we left our camp unguarded. We'll ride down to the valley at once!"

Carol Tinsley felt as though a spell had been broken, and Centaur King no longer bore any resemblance to a small boy who needed mothering. Now he was his old confident self, perfectly poised, and the dominant leader.

"Must you go?" she heard herself ask inanely, knowing what the answer would be.

"You will let us know if we can help in any way," King ignored the question, as he picked up his Stetson.

Rose Tinsley opened the door to the front room and told King that Crag was conscious and asking for him. She took King's two hands and thanked him with a sincerity that made King feel a glow of deep kinship for the wife of Crag Tinsley. Then she led him into the front room, still holding his left hand.

"Here he is, darling," she told the wounded marshal.

"Howdy, Centaur," Tinsley greeted weakly, but he was smiling through the pallor brought about from the loss of the blood. "Wanted to say my thanks for helping old Doc Snyder patch me up. I've been hurt worse than this . . . ."

"I know," King interrupted. "And you stayed in bed longer. So don't hand me that old one about doing a day's work. How you feeling, Marshal?"

"Guilty," Tinsley answered with a twisted smile. "I should have put up more of a fight against that killer, and it will be different next time we meet!"

"Better not talk too much now," King cautioned. "I'll ride over to-morrow and look in on you."

"Won't you wear that star of mine until I get up off bed-ground?" Tinsley pleaded.

"I'm not a Texan," King excused himself. "I know little of the customs here in Lanthrope, and my business is taming horses!"

"I reckon you've tamed most of them hereabouts," Tinsley agreed, and he extended his big right hand. "Well, take care of yourself, *amigo*!"

King shook hands warmly and said he would be careful. Crag Tinsley smiled at Pegasus and told the boy to ride over and see Sugar Foots.

"Yes, Suh, Marshal," Pegasus agreed heartily. "And I hope you will be feeling good pretty soon again."

"I'll be up and around in a week," Tinsley boasted. "If you was just a mite older, Peg, I'd ask you to wear a star until I get on my hind legs again."

"Thank you, Suh," Peg answered soberly. "But I wouldn't make a good law-dog, Suh. I'd want to kill anyone who hurt Centaur!"

"Good-night, Carol, and Mrs. Tinsley," King said slowly, and he backed toward the door.

"It's after eleven," Rose Tinsley said, after glancing at the mantel clock. "Do be careful as

194

you ride down the valley road. And do ride over to-morrow."

Carol Tinsley came to the door and offered her hand to Centaur King. He took it gently, and raised his eyes when the girl tightened her fingers and gripped him like a man.

"Good-night, *amigo*," she said softly.

"*Hasta la vista*," Pegasus said in Spanish, which was customary when old friends expected to meet again soon.

The two climbed their saddles and rode through the darkened town at a walk. Centaur King was silent, but Pegasus was not to be denied.

"*Amigo* means friend," he said, half to himself. "Carol Tinsley called you her *amigo*."

"We will always be friends," King answered shortly.

"That ain't the way that mouthy old Doc put it," Pegasus continued the conversation. "But you put him right back in his place, Centaur!"

Centaur King turned to study the boy, and he remembered that only Madeline's door had separated Pegasus from the kitchen. King wondered how much Pegasus had overheard, and he put out a feeler.

"Old Doc might have a point there," King suggested carelessly. "A man shouldn't be roaming around all his life."

Peg Bronte was silent for a moment as the meaning of King's words sank into his young mind. Then he reacted with the vigour of youth which does not recognize the inhibitions of adult maturity.

"Hog wash!" he blurted contemptuously. "All that talk about a home and a castle might be all right for an old buzzard like him, but you and me are different. We like to travel, and the open road, and we don't want any truck with bossy females!"

Centaur King relaxed in his saddle. With the wind and the night air about him, and a good horse between his knees, he was once more in his own element. One in which he knew most of the answers, and in which there was little of the complicated.

"I reckon you're right, Peg," he agreed. "Unless those bossy females happen to be wild horses," he added.

"That's right," Pegasus agreed, and then he gave King something else to worry about. "When you give a filly an order, that female does what you tell her," Peg added.

King thought for a time, and when he spoke again, his tone was impersonal, and purely conversational.

"Of course, we must recognize that horses and women are different," he set out his bait.

"I wouldn't know about that," Pegasus answered carelessly. "I treat them all the same."

"Nuh uh," King contradicted with a chuckle.

"When Sugar Foots orders you around, you step about lively!"

"Sugar Foots is different," Pegasus defended himself. "She's just a little ole gal-chip, and she cuddles up to a feller like a puppy what needs a friend. Course, when she can't have her way, she starts blubbering, and I 'spise and detest to see a gal crying all over her face."

"Uh huh," King agreed gravely. "But that's just a matter of age, Peg. Now when Sugar Foots gets older, she won't cry so much. She will just look hurt, and she will pout. That makes you feel like you have kicked your pet puppy, but the results are just the same."

"No foolin'?" Peg asked curiously, and then his voice sharpened. "That Miss Carol," he said slowly. "Was she pouting, and acting hurt-like?"

Centaur King started and decided that the matter of the opposite sex had been under personal discussion a bit too long. He nudged Major Domo slyly with a heel, and the big horse leaped into a run. King made a pretence of quieting the horse, and Peg Bronte was busy with Golden. When the horses were brought under control and in an easy lope, Pegasus had forgotten the discussion.

"There's the wagon up ahead, Centaur," he said to his companion. "A fire will feel good after all this rain."

"No fire to-night," King negatived the suggestion, and his hand went down to touch his gun.

"I forgot, Centaur," Pegasus agreed. "With that killer riding gun-sign on both of us, we better make a cold camp."

# CHAPTER FOURTEEN
## THE RANSOM

Centaur King felt a vague uneasiness as he rode toward his Conestoga wagon atop the little knoll. Now it was past midnight, and the air was crisp after the heavy rains. The clouds had cleared some to allow the faint silvery light of a sickle moon to dispel much of the murky darkness which had covered the prairie. King reined to a stop and motioned with his head for Pegasus to ride closer.

"We'll stand a trick apiece of night-herding, Peg," he said to the boy. "I'll stand the graveyard watch, and you take the dog-watch."

"You mean Colt Johnson might be lurking around?" Pegasus asked in a whisper, as he scanned the road on both sides.

"Probably my imagination," King admitted honestly. "I just thought there was no use taking fool chances after what happened to-night. Now here's what we will do. You wait here while I ride up to the wagon. That way we will divide our forces, and thin the target we would make riding in together."

"Let me ride in first, Centaur," Pegasus pleaded. "Then if that killing son makes a play, you can take it up from there!"

"The other way around," King insisted sternly. "If Johnson should make a play, you ride back to Lanthrope and get some help."

"I ought to have me a six-shooter, Centaur," the boy answered hopefully. "I wouldn't go around shooting folks up, or pulling any kid stunts with a hog-leg!"

Centaur King smiled at the boy's eagerness, but he shook his head slowly. "I don't want you to get powder-smoke blood in your veins, Pegasus," he said earnestly. "You've had a touch of it to-night, and it's bound to take something away from you in this profession of taming horses."

"Then you've got powder-smoke in your blood," Pegasus said with finality. "You killed Pete Powers, and you gave the word for Major Domo to kill Al Johnson!"

"That's right," King agreed heavily. "And I feel different than I did before the hold-up. So you wait here in the shadows while I ride up to the wagon alone. I'll whistle to give you the go-ahead if everything is clear. Those are orders!"

"Like you said, Centaur," Peg Bronte answered quietly. "But if Colt Johnson gets you, I'll ride gun-sign on him from now on!"

Centaur King touched Major Domo with a heel and rode down toward the knoll alone. It was foolhardy at best, he told himself, coming back to a deserted camp in the middle of the night,

200

and he studied the shadows of the cottonwoods intently.

He dismounted at the gate and searched the muddy ground for a sign. Then he shook his head and led the black stallion through. The ground was all cut up from the tracks of many horses coming and going, and the light was none too good.

King watched the ears of his horse as he rode up the grade to the little knoll. Major Domo seemed only too glad to be coming back to camp and green feed. The team of bays whinnied a welcome, and King breathed a sigh of relief. He dismounted and stripped his riding gear near the back of the big wagon, watching the horse as he worked. Major Domo would have been quick to detect the presence of a stranger who might be hiding inside the wagon.

Humming carelessly, King threw his heavy saddle in the wagon and picked up a picket rope. When Major Domo was staked out to graze, King whistled three times. Then he climbed into the wagon and made a careful inspection just to be sure.

He was sitting on the tail-gate when Peg Bronte rode through the gate and stopped to close it. He smiled when the boy came into the camp at a dead run, with the duelling pistol in his right hand.

"Light down and rest your saddle," King called

with a grin, and now the pressure of events had left him. "You look disappointed, Peg."

"Come to think of it, he didn't know we were camped here," Peg answered thoughtfully. "I'd like to know how bad he is hurt from that slug of mine!"

"Chances are you missed him," King answered with a yawn. "Strip your gear and picket Golden out on the grass. Put him down toward the gate, and that away we've got a horse on all four sides of the wagon."

"Even an Injun couldn't get past those horses," Peg agreed. "Are you going to let me wear that gun when I stand my trick of sentry go?"

"That's right," King agreed, although he had given no previous thought to it. "Better get busy and turn in. It won't take long to spend the night here as it is."

Peg Bronte unsaddled and staked the golden stallion on the short grass toward the gate. He was still bright-eyed with excitement when he climbed into the wagon and went to his bunk, but King sat on an overturned bucket in the shadows and told the boy to get some sleep.

The horses settled down and started to graze, and the night insects took up their interrupted chant. An hour passed before King heard Peg Bronte breathing deeply to tell him that the healthy youngster had gone to sleep.

Centaur King yawned sleepily and stood up

202

to stretch his legs. The golden stallion jerked up its head and stopped grazing. Then the horse whinnied softly with ears pricked forward.

Centaur King reached inside the wagon and took a thirty gun from a pair of braces which held the rifle in place. His fingers moved swiftly to load the gun, and he cocked his head to listen, wondering if Peg Bronte had awakened. Reassured by the boy's deep breathing, King slipped away from the wagon and took his stand behind a cottonwood facing the gate.

Then he heard the drum of hooves as a rider pounded down the road from the north. King levered a shell into the breech and drew a bead when the horse-backer stopped at the gate. A voice called hoarsely through the gloom, and King recognized Hank White who ran the livery barn in Lanthrope.

"Mister King; it's Hank White calling!"

King lowered his rifle and left the shelter of the gnarled old tree. He called guardedly for White to come up, and then he walked down to meet the horseman.

"You got to come back to town, Centaur!" White almost shouted. "That killer busted into the marshal's house and stole the little gal!"

"No!" Centaur King gasped, and his hands tightened on the rifle. "How about the marshal?"

"Doc Snyder gave Crag something to make him sleep, and he don't know anything about

203

it," White explained. "Rose Tinsley was sitting with the marshal in the front room when she heard the little girl screaming. Rose grabbed the marshal's six-shooter, and Miss Carol ran from her bedroom to see what was going on!"

"Out with it, man!" King said quietly. "Is Miss Carol safe?"

"I dunno," White answered. "Rose Tinsley threatened to shoot Johnson unless he put the little gal down, but that killer had his gun in his fist. He said he'd kill Madeline if Rose made a move, and then he backed toward the back door!"

Centaur King ran to the wagon and hauled out his saddle and bridle. His mind was seething as he ran to Major Domo and led the black stallion to the wagon. Peg Bronte came out rubbing his eyes and stomping into his boots, and the boy heard Hank White tell the rest of the story.

"Seems like Johnson heard about that bank robbery, and he said he means to hold the little gal until he gets the loot. Said he'd kill anyone who followed him, but Miss Carol saddled her horse and rode after the killer. You've got to hurry, King!"

"I should have stayed there!" King blamed himself. "I might have known that killer would have hunted up Crag Tinsley!"

"He even took the marshal's hoss," White added. "I sent one of my hostlers down to Stanhope to get Sheriff Ben Clay, but they can't get back before daylight even if they ride fast!"

Peg Bronte had said nothing, but he was saddling the golden stallion as White told his story. The boy's face was white and drawn in the moonlight, and the duelling pistol was thrust down in the band of his white riding breeches. He dumped some cartridges into his pocket, watched King's face for a moment, and then spoke grimly.

"I'm riding along, Centaur. I'll kill that owl-hooter for what he's done to Sugar Foots!"

"It lacks an hour to daybreak," White murmured. "There should be enough light to read sign by the time we get back to town!"

Centaur King didn't say anything, but the light in his dark eyes was more expressive than words. He mounted his horse, jerked his head toward the gate and Lanthrope, and he tucked the rifle down in the saddle-scabbard under his left leg. After he had closed the gate, he held the stallion to a trot as the three rode back to town.

"Let's hurry, Centaur!" Peg Bronte pleaded. "Every minute might count!"

"Take it easy, Peg," King answered calmly, but his deep voice vibrated to tell of a terrible anger. "We don't know which way that killer rode, and we've got to have daylight to follow the sign Miss Carol must have left."

Pegasus scowled fiercely and muttered threats below his breath. They came to the edge of town and rode to the end of the main street reaching

Crag Tinsley's house just as the first fingers of dawn were breaking through the eastern sky.

Rose Tinsley came through the kitchen door with her husband's gunbelt strapped around her waist. She ran to King and seized his hand, but she was not crying, and her voice was low and strong as she spoke to the horse tamer.

"You'll save Madeline, Centaur King?" she pleaded. "We've got three thousand dollars in the bank, and we will give every bit of it to Colt Johnson if he will give Madeline back to us!"

"We will save her, Mrs. Tinsley," King answered confidently. "You stay here with Crag, and try not to worry."

He handed his bridle reins to Peg Bronte as he began to search the ground back by the low barn. Hank White joined him and pointed to some deep horse-shoe marks just outside the barn.

"Those tracks were made by the marshal's hoss, King," the livery man said jubilantly. "Crag had me put calks on those front shoes, and they are heading back toward the Sandias!"

"What kind of a horse?" King asked.

"He's a big strawberry roan," White replied. "Miss Carol's hoss is a chestnut with white stockings in front. I'll ride along on account of I know the country back in them low hills."

Centaur King told Rose Tinsley they would be back as soon as they had news, and the three rode toward the distant foothills. Hank White said it was fifteen miles to the Sandias, and King asked him for a description of Colt Johnson.

"He's a lathy hombre crowding six feet," White answered. "About thirty years old with buck teeth. He talks in a high voice, and I wouldn't trust him with snow water and let him melt it hisself!"

King nodded as he followed the trail of the desperate fugitive. Now they were in brushy country, but White knew all the trails. They stopped at a fork in the trail as the sun came out strong, and Centaur King pointed to a second set of tracks which now joined the first.

"Carol found the trail here," King said slowly. "I don't know what she expected to do alone, against a desperate killer."

Peg Bronte tugged at King's arm and pointed up the trail. A rider was coming toward them, and that rider was a woman. Carol Tinsley galloped up and came straight to Centaur King.

"I knew you'd come, Centaur," she said with a wan smile. "Colt Johnson is holed up in Painted Cave, and I believe he has been using it for a hide-out!"

"He could stand off an army there," Hank White said nervously. "And he probably has plenty of provisions!"

Centaur King was watching the girl's face, and he reached out and pressed her hand. He told her quietly not to worry, and to lead the way to

Painted Cave. Hank White added that the sheriff and his posse should get there by noon, and they started up the gradually rising trail.

Now they were in the low sandy hills which were covered with scrub oak and catclaw. Carol Tinsley was in the lead, and she reined in and signalled for a stop at the foot of a steep trail.

"Painted Cave is at the top," she whispered to King. "He must have seen us coming!"

"Stop where you are!" a high-pitched voice commanded loudly, and Centaur King glanced around in an effort to find the speaker.

"That nest of rocks yonder," Hank White whispered hoarsely. "We call them the Whispering Rocks. I've done it many's the time when I was a button. You can talk up there in the cave, and it carries your voice down there to those rocks!"

"Does it carry back?" King asked quietly.

"Yeah," White answered, with a nod of his head. "And it must be all of a quarter of a mile up there to the cave."

King rode over to the nest of rocks and studied the formation. Evidently the hill was honeycombed by small tunnels made by erosion, and he dismounted and walked into the circle of rocks.

"We heard you, Johnson," he said clearly. "If you hurt the little girl, you'll answer to me. This is Centaur King!"

"You can wait, hoss tamer," the snarling answer

came out of the rocks. "There was eight thousand dollars in that bank loot, and I want it. If I don't get it, Crag Tinsley will never see his kid again!"

"Ask him if Madeline is safe?" Carol whispered, and Peg Bronte edged us close.

"Madeline," King spoke clearly. "Is she all right?"

"I want to come home," a childish voice pleaded tearfully. "I don't like this bad man!"

"You hurt Sugar Foots and I'll kill you, Colt Johnson!" Peg Bronte screamed at the hole in the rocks. "I won't miss you next time!"

Silence for a moment, and then the high-pitched voice spoke venomously. "So you're the button who cut down on me from the dark. I won't be forgetting!"

"Save me, Peggie!" the little girl's voice pleaded. "Come up and get me, Peggie!"

"You come up here and I'll whittle another notch on my gun!" Colt Johnson threatened grimly, and King pulled the boy away from the hole in the rocks.

"About that money, Johnson," King spoke clearly. "If you get it, will you release the little girl?"

"Now you're talking sense," the answer came from the hole. "Send that salty hairpin up with the loot, and you can have the brat!"

Carol Tinsley sighed as her eyes filled with tears. Centaur King turned his eyes away from the girl, and now his face was hard and stern. Only that glowing light in his eyes told of his anger, and it burned savagely as he spoke again.

"I'll bring the money myself, Johnson. How do I know you won't pull a trick?"

"I'll get you later, King," the answer came promptly. "Right now I want that money!"

"But we don't have that eight thousand dollars," Carol spoke up hopelessly. "And he will kill you, Centaur!"

"I have the money here in my saddle-bags," King said with a shrug. "Money is the cheapest thing in the world, and you can't take it with you."

Pegasus Bronte stared with a question in his wide eyes. "But, Centaur," he argued. "The sheriff took that bank loot back to Stanhope with him."

Centaur King frowned and stepped up to the hole in the rocks which was just about shoulder-high. His voice was firm with decision when he spoke to the outlaw in the cave.

"I have the eight thousand, Johnson. Now it's up to you to say the word. You won't get the money unless Madeline is delivered to me unharmed!"

"And you won't get the kid until I get the money!" the outlaw shouted back.

"I'll bring the money halfway," King answered calmly. "You bring Madeline down halfway. If you pull a trick, Peg Bronte will kill you. If I pull one, you can kill either the child or me before we can get back to cover!"

Silence for a time, and then the outlaw spoke again, and now his voice was low and deadly. "It's a deal, King. But I'm warning you that I will keep my gun on the kid all the time. If you get me, I'll get the kid!"

"You heard the agreement, Peg," King said to the boy. "I want you to cover the trail with the rifle, but you know what will happen if you go to fighting your head."

He reached to his saddle-bags and pulled out a canvas sack bulging with currency and gold. Then he loosed the six-shooter in his holster; the gun that had belonged to the brother of Colt Johnson. With a smile at Carol, Centaur King stepped out of the circle of rocks and began to climb the long steep trail.

Pegasus took his position behind a low rock and sighted the rifle up the trail. Carol Tinsley knelt beside the boy, and Hank White muttered softly as he scanned the upper trail.

"Yonder he comes!" White said hoarsely. "And Madeline is with him!"

Peg Bronte fined his sights on the outlaw, and his dark eyes narrowed to slits. His lips worked silently, and Carol spoke gently.

"Sugar Foots is safe, Peg. Please be careful!"

Centaur King was climbing the trail with the

canvas sack in his left hand. He saw Colt Johnson step out holding the little girl by one hand. His cocked six-shooter was in the other, and a spare rode in the holster on the outlaw's left leg.

Closer and closer the two men came, watching each other warily. They met on a little level shelf halfway up the trail. Centaur King handed the sack to the outlaw, and took Madeline's hand.

Colt Johnson shook the sack and stared at the money. His pistol covered the little girl, and King had his first good look at the desperate killer.

"I needed the money," Johnson said in a snarl. "I've kept my part of this bargain, but let me tell you something, King. You killed my brother and Pete Powers, and I'll kill you if it takes the rest of my life!"

"Name the time and place," King said quietly. "Or do you mean you'd rather sneak and hide, and shoot me in the back?"

"You'll get an even break, if it falls that away," Johnson said savagely. "I've got you beat, and we both know it."

"Any time you say," King agreed, and taking Madeline's hand in a firm grip, he started down the trail.

Colt Johnson backed up, and his pistol still covered the little girl who was unconscious of danger. Centaur King did not turn his head, and if he felt any fear, it did not show in his stern features. Madeline was strangely silent, but when she saw Pegasus Bronte, she left King and ran to the boy.

Peg grabbed the child in his arms and ducked behind a tall boulder. Colt Johnson had disappeared, and now little Madeline was sobbing as she clung to Peg Bronte.

"I knew you'd come, Peggie!" she told the boy.

"Sure, Sugar Foots," Pegasus said gruffly. "Now you quit that blubberin' and give me a big kiss. You hear me, Sugar?"

His answer was a tearful kiss, and Carol Tinsley went to Centaur King. She swayed toward him, and King put his arms around her.

"Thanks, Centaur," she said simply. "I, too, knew you would come!"

# CHAPTER FIFTEEN
## THE CHALLENGE

Hank White scratched his stubbled chin as he tried to appear interested in Painted Cave while letting on not to see the romance unfolding before his eyes. Centaur King dropped his arms and pressed Carol's hand as he smiled.

"Somebody ought to stay here and keep that swamp coon cooped up there in the cave until Sheriff Clay gets here," the livery man suggested. "That money won't do him nary bit of good where he is, and Ben Clay won't leave the trail until he puts the hobbles on Johnson."

"You mean you want to guard this trail?" King asked expectantly.

"That's right," White agreed. "I know you didn't get a wink of sleep last night, nor Miss Carol either. The sheriff and his posse should be here soon, and once that old law-hound has treed a varmint, he won't leave until he smokes his out, or Colt Johnson surrenders."

"My regards to the sheriff, and tell him he can get in touch with me through the Tinsleys," King replied, and now he showed a trace of weariness.

"Yeah, well I'll be seeing you," a high-pitched voice spoke from the rocks.

Centaur King frowned. He had forgotten the acoustics of Whispering Rocks, and Carol Tinsley was wide-eyed with fear. King stared thoughtfully at the nest of rocks and then spoke calmly.

"Perhaps I'll be seeing you, Johnson. That is, unless you try to dry-gulch me like you did the marshal."

"I'll rattle before I strike," the answer came back through the rocks. "I noticed you were wearing my brother's gun. Right now you've got a hand on it. Mebbe Al can hear me, and I'm promising him to whittle your notch on my own!"

Pegasus Bronte listened and glanced at King. The horse tamer was gripping the captured gun, and Peg spoke curiously.

"You reckon he can see us down here, Centaur?"

Centaur King smiled tolerantly. "He just made a good guess," he told the boy "Any man touches his gun when another man threatens him. Right now Colt Johnson is gripping both his guns, with his lips skinned back over his buck teeth!"

A snarling curse whispered through the rocks to tell that King had scored a bull's-eye. The horse tamer jerked his head down toward the trail where they had left the horses, and thanking Hank White, King led the way with Carol Tinsley.

Peg Bronte was carrying Madeline who clung tightly with her chubby arms around the boy's neck. Now that she was out of danger, Pegasus was again delivering a lecture.

"Looky, Sugar Foots," he scolded. "I'm goin' to warp you a few if you don't quit callin' me Peggie. You hear my wau-wau?"

"Yes, Pegasus," Madeline answered soberly, and King pressed Carol's arm as he grinned.

"We must get right back and let Rose know that Madeline is safe," Carol whispered, and then she stopped and stared at King. "That eight thousand dollars you gave Colt Johnson," she said slowly. "Peg said that you gave the bank loot to Sheriff Clay."

"Sometimes Peg just talks to hear the wind blow," King answered lightly. "There might be a little squall," he continued. "But I better take Madeline with me on Major Domo. Golden has not been broken long enough to carry double, especially such a precious burden as Sugar Foots."

"I want to ride with Peggie," Madeline wailed.

"I can make out, Centaur," Pegasus argued. "Gold 'Un won't go to fighting his head."

"It isn't that, Peg," King explained. "It's all of fifteen miles back to town, and a lot of it is downhill over twisting hairpin trails. Tell you what! I'll take her until we are out of the hills, and then you take over from there."

"Keno," Pegasus agreed, after King had mounted the black stallion, the boy handed Madeline to the horse tamer.

217

The little girl put her arms around King's neck and hugged him tight. "Thanks for coming to get me, Centaur," she said gravely.

"Madeline," Carol corrected. "You must say Mister King!"

"Peggie calls him Centaur," the child pouted.

"Wham her one for me, Centaur," Peg Bronte said with a scowl. "She went and called me 'Peggie' again!"

King tightened his arms and kissed Madeline on the cheek. "I'll be mighty proud if she calls me Centaur," he said happily. "Now you take cowboys for instance. When they go around calling a man 'Mister,' you know without telling that they don't like that fellow. You just call me Centaur, Sugar."

Carol Tinsley smiled and admitted defeat. Peg Bronte mounted Golden and brought up the drag. They started back to town through the head-high buckthorn, and after a few minutes, King announced that his charge was fast asleep.

"She's a brave little somebody," he told Carol. "Snatched up out of her bed and carted off to the wild hills in her night clothes, and she isn't making any fuss about it."

"Crag and Rose have only three thousand in the bank," Carol said with a sigh. "I have as much more, and we will pay the balance with interest!"

"You owe me nothing," King answered quickly. "Please, Carol, promise me not to make us both uncomfortable about something which has given me a great deal of happiness."

"Crag won't have it that way," Carol said quietly.

"Hasn't Crag got enough to worry about right now?" King asked. "Would you protest if I wanted to tame just one wild horse if it would save little Madeline's life?"

"You know I wouldn't, Centaur," the girl answered without hesitation. "But you didn't tame one wild horse to save Madeline. You risked your life, and you gave your own money!"

"It was down in New Orleans," King said musingly. "A plantation owner had a big savage Blennerhasset stallion. He was a killer by the name of Black Devil. The owner bet me ten thousand that I couldn't enter a box stall with the horse and gentle the beast. It took me just twenty minutes, and I won that bet!"

Carol Tinsley sighed and tightened her lips. Centaur King looked uncomfortable, and he glanced reproachfully at Peg Bronte who had blurted out the news about the return of the bank loot to Sheriff Clay.

Pegasus grinned at the older man, and winked impudently at Carol Tinsley. "Don't fash yourself none about that money, Miss Carol," he told the girl. "You heard Centaur make a date with Colt Johnson, and after he smokes that outlaw down, Centaur will take back his money!"

"Pegasus!" King said sternly. "That will do from you!"

"Yes, Suh, Centaur," the boy answered quietly. "But ain't I right, Centaur?"

"Now when we get back to town, you bridle your jaw," King warned the boy. "Or I'll make you hard to find!"

"I won't talk with my big mouth wide open, Centaur," Pegasus promised soberly. "Sorry if I talked out of turn, pard."

"I know you are, and it's all right," King answered with a warm smile. "But we don't want to worry Crag or Rose."

They rode along in silence as the trails became steeper. The sun was climbing high when they reached the lower valley, and Peg Bronte rode alongside of King and said he'd take the little girl. The golden stallion was behaving perfectly, and King handed Madeline to the eager boy. Then he dropped back to rub stirrups with Carol Tinsley.

"I don't know what we would have done without you and Pegasus," the girl murmured gratefully. She was quiet for a moment, and then she raised her head and looked squarely at King.

"Are you really going through with it?" she asked in a whisper.

"Of course," King answered heartily. "As soon as we can, we will work in Stanhope."

"You are evading the issue, Centaur," the girl

scolded. "Are you going to meet Colt Johnson?"

"*Quien sabe*?" King answered with a shrug. "Who knows?"

"You know," the girl persisted. "You sounded eager to meet Colt Johnson for a pistol duel!"

"You forget that he has threatened to kill me," King reminded the girl. "Stop and think a moment, Carol. Crag was shot without warning. I asked only for an even break. I'm not afraid of anything I can see!"

"Then you do intend to meet him," Carol said faintly.

"Yes," King admitted honestly. "If he does not find me, I will search for him!"

"If I asked you not to?"

"But you wouldn't," King said with confidence. "You would know that you were taking from me my right of self-defence, and you would not do that."

"No, I wouldn't," Carol agreed with a sigh. "Perhaps the sheriff will capture him," she said hopefully.

"Colt Johnson will never surrender," King said slowly. "He's as treacherous as a rattler, and just as venomous. He almost succeeded in killing your brother, and now he has taken a vow to get both Peg and me."

"Perhaps if you went to California," the girl suggested, but King shook his dark head vigorously.

"No man ever escaped trouble by running away," he said quietly. "And I never was much of a hand at running away."

"You wouldn't do it for me?"

"I'd do most anything for you, Carol," King answered with simple sincerity. "You know how I feel about you, but I could not live comfortably without honour!"

"But I don't know how you feel about me," Carol contradicted, but she turned her face to hide the gleam of happiness in her brown eyes.

"Some time I will tell you," Centaur King promised, and he smiled to show his dazzling white teeth. "I haven't seen those paintings you did of Peg and Golden," he changed the subject.

"I also made one of you and Major Domo," Carol told him, but somehow she seemed disappointed. "I've been thinking of taking a trip when Crag is out of bed," she continued. "We could get a good wagon, and I could paint some pictures as we travelled."

"Perhaps we could travel together," King suggested eagerly. "If Crag and Rose really want to take a trip."

"Rose does, but it would take more than wild horses to drag Crag away from his job now," Carol said pensively. "And he will need a long rest after he recovers from his wounds."

"I've been thinking," King said suddenly. "Either Peg or myself should stay at your house until Crag gets up and about. We could take turns about, and still get our gear ready for the Stanhope work."

"You haven't changed your mind about settling here?" the girl asked hopefully.

King frowned before answering. "My work is where I find it," he explained patiently. "I have made it my profession, as you have made the painting of pictures your life work."

"Is it the work, or the thrill you get from taming wild horses?" Carol asked directly.

"Both," King answered without hesitation. "It's simply a case of me enjoying my work, and when I am not training horses, something is lacking which robs me of content."

"Are you always going to train horses?" Carol asked quietly.

Centaur King nodded. "Are you always going to paint pictures?" he countered.

"But painting is different," the girl argued. "One can keep house, and still paint pictures."

"One can keep house, and still train horses," King answered, and to him the answer was logical.

"You mean keep house in a wagon?" Carol asked, and now her voice was a bit sharp.

"You know, I've thought about that," King said musingly. "Peg and I love the open road. I toyed with the idea that perhaps later I would settle down in a home of my own. Stay there through the winter, and then go on the road in the spring and summer."

"I am glad Pegasus is growing," Carol said with a smile. "It will be so much nicer and more dignified when he beats the drum with the stallion following him!"

"It will be nice," King agreed. "We have talked about it, and Peg is learning fast. When he masters the double roll and gets Golden trained, we will have a double feature which will surely attract the crowds!"

Carol leaned back in her saddle and stared at his handsome face. She knew that he had reproved her without even mentioning her dislike for his showmanship. He had also told her that he had no intention of changing, and Carol Tinsley's little chin set stubbornly.

"I'm sure you and Pegasus will make a successful team," she said coldly.

"Yes, we have hit it off from the start," King agreed. "See how carefully he holds Madeline?"

"He thinks a lot of her in his funny way," Carol admitted. "And you think a lot of Pegasus," she added.

Centaur King turned quickly at the note of jealousy in her low throaty voice. He watched her for a long moment before he spoke, and then he spoke plainly.

"I do," he replied. "I have no plans which do not include Pegasus."

"We are almost home," Carol changed the subject abruptly. "I don't believe it will be necessary for us to have a guard at the house," she added coldly.

Centaur King appeared older as he turned his head.

"Very well," he answered. "You do not need a guard, but Crag and Madeline do. When Crag is on his feet again, Peg and I will resume our trip."

"Of course, if you insist on staying," Carol said coldly.

"I do," King answered. "I will try not to bother you, Miss Carol."

"I will be busy with my painting, Mister King," Carol retorted, and then they were in front of the marshal's house.

Centaur King dismounted and held out his arms for the little girl. He took her gently, and Peg Bronte whispered that his right arm had gone to sleep. Rose Tinsley came running from the house, and King handed the little girl to her mother.

"My baby!" Rose Tinsley sobbed, and then Madeline awoke and appeared startled. She started to wail for Peggie, and then she realized that she was in her mother's arms.

"I missed you, Mummy," Madeline whispered. "And I missed my Daddy. How is Daddy, Mummy?"

"Lots better now," Rose answered happily.

"Come, darling; your Daddy wants to see you. Please come in, Centaur and Peg."

"Just for a moment," King answered.

Rose Tinsley ran in the house with Madeline, and when King entered through the kitchen, the marshal was propped up with pillows. He extended a hand to the horse tamer and his voice was gruff as he voiced his thanks.

"I'll never forget what you've done for me and mine, Centaur," Crag Tinsley said gratefully.

"The ransom!" Rose asked breathlessly. "He demanded the eight thousand dollars taken from the bank!"

"We gave it to him," King admitted. "We found him in the Painted Cave, and we made a deal."

"So we owe Mister King eight thousand dollars," Carol interrupted. "He paid Colt Johnson with his own money!"

Centaur King showed his distress, but Pegasus was not to be denied. He faced Carol with anger flashing in his brown eyes, and his voice was harsh when he lashed at her.

"You heard what Centaur said, Miss Carol. He said it made him happy to do what he did for Sugar Foots, and you don't owe him anything!"

"What's this?" Rose Tinsley asked slowly, but King was glaring at the boy.

"You will make your manners, Peg?" King asked quietly.

"I won't!" Peg Bronte shouted. "You go up

226

there under that killer's gun, and then she quarrels with you all the way home on account |of you want to beat the skins when we go into a new town!"

"That will do," King said sternly. "You go out and stay with the horses, Pegasus. Folks, I'm sorry Pegasus talked out of turn," King apologized humbly.

"We won't accept any apology," Crag Tinsley said bluntly. "Peg is right, and him only a button. Did you say something, Sis?"

"I'm sorry if I appeared ungrateful, Mister King," Carol Tinsley said in a low voice. "If you will excuse me now, I will go to my room."

Centaur King watched the girl with a deep misery in his dark eyes. Pegasus came slowly to him and lowered his head.

"I got a hoss-whupping a-coming, pard," he said just above a whisper. "I'll feel better after I get it."

Centaur King smiled and placed an arm about Peg Bronte's shoulders. His fingers viced down hard on the boy's arm, and then he smiled wistfully.

"Looks like you will have to suffer, pard," he told Pegasus. "When was the last time you remember me flogging you?"

"You never did," Peg whispered. "But I had it coming many's a time."

"Don't ever let anything come between you and

that boy, Centaur," the marshal advised softly. "He's all true metal!"

"I'll tell a man," King agreed. "Now we will be getting back to our camp in the valley, and make up a little sleep. Take it easy, Crag, and make him stay quiet, Rose."

Rose Tinsley followed them to the door, drew King aside, and spoke in a whisper.

"Carol is tired, and under a strain, Centaur. She's the dearest girl in the world, and after she sleeps on this little disagreement, she will be different. Thank you and Peg so much!"

# CHAPTER SIXTEEN
## THE ESCAPE

Lanthrope was seething with angry ranchers who had come to town for a man-hunt. Word had spread about the kidnapping of little Madeline Tinsley, and the shooting of her father, the marshal.

Centaur King rode down the street with Pegasus, and they saw the crowd gathered in Dapper Jim Stacey's sales ring. Scores of horses were tied to the rails, and the auctioneer had a heavy six-shooter strapped around his lean hips, under his checkered, cut-away coat. Stacey saw King coming, and walked out to beckon.

Centaur King frowned and reined toward the corrals. He and Peg Bronte had intended getting dinner in town before riding down to their valley camp, and he would have preferred not meeting the townspeople at this time. A glow came to his heart when he saw the sincere friendship written on the rugged faces of the ranchers as they greeted him and Peg.

"Light down and rest your saddle, Centaur," Stacey urged the weary horse tamer. "No rush about getting back to your camp. I sent one of my men down to look after your stock, and we all owe you a debt we can never repay!"

"Any one of you would have done the same," King said slowly. "I just played the cards the way they were dealt to me."

"Yeah," Stacey murmured. "And Colt Johnson will deal you the Ace of Spades off the bottom of the pack!"

"Perhaps not," King answered with a careless shrug. "How about Sheriff Ben Clay?"

"He rode up there to Painted Cave an hour ago," Stacey answered. "Had a posse of six men, but we've got forty here. We are going to comb the hills until we get Johnson!"

"Good luck, and good hunting," King said cheerily. "Now Peg and me are going to get down to camp and make up our sleep."

"That's right, you were up all night," Stacey said, and he showed his disappointment. "I was going to ask you and Peg to ride with us, but I know how you feel. Take care of yourself, man."

King thanked Stacey, nodded to the ranchers, and turned his black stallion to ride out of the yard. They stopped at a little restaurant and ordered food. Both ate hungrily and without much talk. Peg Bronte also showed weariness, and now that Madeline was safe, the boy was glad that they were going back to camp.

King smiled and nodded to show his appreciation when they reached the camp and found the team had been fed, and the harness nicely cleaned and oiled. After picketing the two stallions, they undressed and sought their bunks in the roomy wagon.

The sun was a coppery disc in the distant west when King yawned and opened his eyes. For a long moment he lay without moving, but his yawn had awakened Pegasus. The boy slid his legs out of the bunk and pulled on his riding pants.

"Morning, pard," he greeted King. "I slept like a log."

"We are falling into strange habits, Peg," King answered thoughtfully. "Here it is almost seven o'clock in the evening, and you bid me a bright and cheery good-morning."

"I'll stir us up a bait of hot grub," Peg suggested.

"While I look around," King agreed, as he began to dress.

Peg Bronte nodded approvingly when King strapped on the now familiar belt and gun. He busied himself with a fire while King took a turn through the cottonwood grove. Jim Stacey's man had even filled the wooden tubs with water from the creek, and had dumped about a ton of prairie hay near the wagon.

King smiled when Peg Bronte called him for "breakfast." The boy had prepared bacon and eggs, hot cakes and black-strap, and steaming cowboy coffee.

"You're in a rut, Peg," he accused the bright-eyed boy. "No matter what time of the day or night we get up after sleeping, you always cook breakfast."

"I cooked what I had to cook, Mister King," Peg answered with quiet dignity. "The way we've been sky-hootin' around, when did you last go to the store for provisions, may I ask?"

"I had it coming," King admitted with a chuckle, and once more he felt contented and relaxed. "There's no place like home," he commented. "Even if it is only a wagon and a camp."

"Pay no mind to that filly, Centaur," Peg advised loyally. "She would like to hobble you down to a house in town, but you won't never stay put that away."

King glanced up with a startled expression. Then he realized that Peg Bronte had overheard most of his conversation with Carol Tinsley, and a faint flush stained the horse tamer's tanned cheeks.

"You meant what you told her, Centaur?" Peg asked slowly.

"I reckon I did, Peg," King drawled. "Just what did I say that cankers you?"

"About you not having any plans that didn't include me," Peg followed up the thought which was fretting him.

Centaur King frowned and stared at the fire. "I meant it, pard," he answered finally. "I think a lot of Miss Carol," he admitted honestly. "No use of me telling you I don't."

"She thinks a heap of you, Centaur," Peg said. "Sometimes I like her, and sometimes I don't. When she talks about you not beating the skins, or settling down, I don't like her so good!"

"I don't believe I ever told you, Peg," King said slowly. For a moment he hesitated as the boy watched him expectantly. "I've got a nice farm back in the Blue Grass country," he continued.

"Back in Kentucky?" Peg asked, his eyes wide with interest. "You got any racehorses on the spread?"

"Quite a few," King answered with a smile. "It's beautiful country, Peg. It belonged to my grandfather, and I bought it back a few years ago."

"Why don't we take a trip back there?" Peg asked eagerly. "After we get back from California and Montana," he amended.

"I was thinking about it," King admitted, but he wasn't looking at the boy.

Peg Bronte studied the handsome face and his own grew long. Now a resentful glow showed in his dark eyes, and his tone was sullen when he spoke to break the silence.

"I know," he said in a low whisper. "You was thinking about going back there with Miss Carol Tinsley. Like as not there's a big house on the place in the Blue Grass, and a dozen servants. Miss Carol would like that there!"

"I'm sure she would," King answered, and then

he jerked around to study the sullen boy. "That's what I mean, Peg," he said gently. "You and I will always be partners, and if I went back, you'd go along."

"I don't want to go back home," Peg drawled. "I want to stay out here in the west!"

"Look at me, Pegasus!" King said sternly.

"I know what you look like," Peg Bronte grumbled.

"Peg," King said gently. "Look at me when I am talking to you, feller. Have I ever lied to you?"

"No you never," Peg admitted grudgingly, and he glanced up to meet King's eyes. "Dadburn it, Centaur!" he burst out. "We was getting along fine, and that Miss Carol upset all our plans!"

"Nuh uh," King contradicted softly. "She just don't know our ways, but she is honest and fine!"

"Mebbe to you, but I don't want no truck with women," Peg commented sulkily. "She wants to own you!"

"Not really," King said patiently. "Let me put it this way, Peg. Now you take those two stallions out yonder. Both of 'em pretty much one-man hosses. Do you own Golden?"

"You dad-gummed right!" the boy answered quickly.

"I see that you have missed the big lesson," King said slowly. "You never own a horse or a dog, Pegasus. They own you, and nothing can make them think differently."

Peg Bronte sat up straight and stared at his mentor. His lips were parted to show his surprise, and he scratched his tousled head uncertainly.

"Mebbe I don't understand all I know," he said in his slow drawl. "You mean Gold 'Un thinks I belong to him, and not the other way around?"

"That's what I mean," King agreed. "You and I both know that Major Domo and Golden could kill us both if they tried. They don't try because they love us, and because we belong to them!"

"Gosh, Centaur, I see what you mean," Peg murmured. "I can see it now the way Gold 'Un rubs his head again my shoulder. When he nuzzles my cheek, and stays close to me out on the trail!"

"Yeah," King answered lazily, as the dusky twilight closed in. "And you just remember how Golden left Miss Carol down there by the creek, and came a-faunching to you. That was because he picked you out for his boss, and because you belonged to him."

"I see what you mean, Centaur," Peg said happily, and then his face clouded again. "What's all this got to do with Miss Carol?" he demanded truculently.

"Women are possessive," King explained slowly. "Men are too, for that matter," he added. "But most times women show it more than men do."

"I'll tell the world," Pegasus agreed dryly.

"They own you body and soul, lock, stock and barrel!"

"They don't," King corrected. "It just appears that away, but when a woman really loves a man, if she is the right kind, she wants her man to be happy, and to do the things which make him happy!"

Peg Bronte pouted his lips, started to speak, and then suddenly changed his mind. Centaur King watched the boy's expressive face with a smile, knowing what Peg was thinking.

"You were saying?" he prompted quietly.

"I wasn't," Peg answered sharply. "I was thinking, but when a man gets older, sometimes he only *thinks!*"

"Right," King agreed. "But when a man gets along in years, he does not allow all his thoughts to show plainly on his face."

Peg Bronte glanced at King suspiciously. "I reckon you read my mind?" he challenged.

"I did," King answered with a nod. "You were thinking what Miss Carol said about me settling down, forsaking the road, and especially about beating the drum with Major Domo prancing at my heels."

"Well, I'm something I wouldn't let no one else call me," Peg whispered. "I cert'ny am. How'd you know, Centaur?"

"I was just reading sign," King answered lazily. "You had it written all over your face, just as

236

Colt Johnson had murder written all over his."

"Yeah," Peg whispered, and then he glanced around the camp. "You reckon that son will keep his promise, Centaur?"

"I have a feeling that he will," King answered gravely but he did not seem perturbed.

"You ain't so good at that trick yourself," Peg Bronte accused. "Right now it's written all over your face that you're anxious to meet up with that killer again, and when you do, it will be through powder-smoke!"

Centaur King appeared startled, but he nodded slowly. "That's reading sign, Peg," he admitted honestly. "I have no personal feeling against Colt Johnson, any more than I have with a deadly snake."

"But if a deadly snake struck at you, you'd kill it," Peg pursued his thought.

"I would," King answered quietly, but now his dark eyes were glowing with that strange light Peg Bronte had noticed when King was aroused.

"The horses are rested," Peg said quietly. "They can rest some more in the marshal's barn!"

"Correction," King answered slowly. "Major Domo can rest in the marshal's barn, but one of us should stay here with the wagon."

"It's that Miss Carol," Peg burst out stormily. "I'm in the way when you talk to her, and you're trying to shake me!"

Centaur King arose and placed both strong

hands on the boy's slender shoulders. He gazed down at Peg Bronte until the boy raised his head defiantly and glared into King's face.

"Stop fighting your head, Peg," King said gently. "You stop and think a moment. The marshal is down on bed-ground with his head under him. Miss Carol does not want to talk to me now and you know it. Well?"

Peg Bronte studied King's face in the fading light. He swallowed noisily, blinked rapidly, and extended his right hand.

"Sorry I acted like a brat, Centaur," he said penitently. "I'll stay and watch the camp, and you guard Madeline and the marshal!"

"Spoken like a man, Pegasus," King thanked the boy. "And I'll be back by sun-up!"

"I've got the rifle and one of the duelling pistols," Peg answered soberly. "Get on with your snake-killing, pard. If you get that rattler under your sights, crack down on him!"

"I won't miss," King assured the boy, and taking his good saddle from the wagon, he carried it over where the black stallion was whickering eagerly.

"You want to be on the go, don't you, boy?" King said to the horse, and then he brushed Major Domo until the black coat glistened. The light was gone by the time he had cinched his saddle, and Peg Bronte was kicking out the fire without being told. The boy waved as King rode down the trail toward town, after which he brushed the golden stallion and returned to the wagon.

Centaur King held his horse to a trot on the way back to Lanthrope. He skirted town to avoid acquaintances, arriving at the marshal's house about eight. Rose Tinsley came to the kitchen door as King rode around toward the barn, and King told her he was going to stable Major Domo and would return to the house.

In the darkness of the barn, King stripped his riding gear and turned the stallion loose in a box stall. Without even a halter, he knew that a stranger could not get near the stallion. Then he walked slowly to the house and Rose met him at the kitchen door.

"Come in, Centaur," she invited cordially. "I know we will all feel better, but you shouldn't lose your sleep just to guard us."

King removed his Stetson and entered the kitchen. Rose told him that Crag was asleep, as well as Madeline. She explained that she and Carol had moved the little girl's bed to the front room with her father, and King glanced around slowly.

"Carol retired early," Rose Tinsley told him.

"Of course," King agreed. "She was up all last night, and she did look tired."

"You seem rested," Rose remarked, and King told her that he had slept all afternoon.

"Keep the house locked," King advised. "I'll

stay close to the barn where I can watch the house."

Rose Tinsley shuddered. "Do you think that . . . that killer will come down here?" she asked with a shudder.

"Have you seen Sheriff Ben Clay?" King asked.

"That's what I mean," the marshal's wife explained, and her voice told of her fears. "Colt Johnson escaped from the Painted Cave. There was a rough trail out the back way no one knew about. They found where his horse had slid down the back trail, and then they lost the trail in the badlands!"

"I had a feeling," King said quietly, and his fingers carelessly touched the handles of his holstered gun. "But now you turn in and don't worry. I will get back to my camp at sun-up, but no one will get past me to-night."

"We are so grateful," Rose thanked him, and King put on his hat and left by the kitchen door. After waiting to hear Rose lock the door, King walked to the barn and sat on his heels with his back against the rough boards.

An hour later the lights were extinguished in the house, and all was still except for the night noises. Centaur King thought of many things as he maintained his solitary vigil. Of the farm back in Kentucky, the future of Pegasus Bronte, and the unpredictable behaviour of the opposite sex. He had not taken time to shave, and a black stubble of beard covered the lower part of his face.

"I'll shave the first thing in the morning," he promised himself, as he rubbed a hand over the bristles. "I hope Peg gets a good night's sleep. He's young, and he needs his rest."

The hours droned away, and King drew the fine watch from his pocket. He held it to his ear, pressed a little knob, and listened. A tiny bell tolled off the hour of midnight, and King stretched slowly to his feet when he saw two dark shapes coming up the street from town.

Keeping to the shadows, King made his way toward the street. He recognized Dapper Jim Stacey who was carrying his stock whip. King called guardedly and went to meet the two men.

"Howdy, King," the second man whispered, and King recognized Ben Clay, the sheriff.

"We saw you riding up the back way about dark," Stacey explained. "You heard about Colt Johnson giving us the slip?"

"Rose told me," King answered. "Any trace of him?"

"Nary," the sheriff answered glumly. "But I mean to stay on his trail until I get him."

"Meantime, we figured you ought to be with the boy in your camp," Stacey took up the talk. "Ben and I will stand guard here, but you better get back in the valley."

"With you both here, I'll do that," King agreed,

241

and the three men walked silently to the barn. "Little Madeline is in the front room with Crag," he told them in a whisper. "Keep a close watch, because the two women didn't get any sleep last night, and will probably sleep soundly."

King entered the barn, speaking softly to the black stallion. He slipped the bridle on first, and led the horse from the stall. Carol Tinsley's horse whinnied eagerly, but King quieted the bay with a whispered word. Then he cinched his saddle securely and led Major Domo from the barn.

"Watch your back, King!" the sheriff warned grimly. "Colt Johnson is a desperate killer, and he won't give you a chance!"

"Don't worry about me," King answered quietly. "Come daylight, I'm going to look around for a sign. I can't get accustomed to dodging and hiding."

"We'll get him to-day, or run him out of the country," Sheriff Clay promised. "We'll start the biggest manhunt to-morrow this County ever saw. And King?"

"Yes, Sheriff?"

"About those rewards," the sheriff said slowly. "If I turn that money over to Crag Tinsley, he could pay his debts!"

"What debts?" King asked tersely.

"That eight thousand is going to worry Crag when he finds out," Jim Stacey said bluntly.

242

"It does not worry me," King answered, with a trace of resentment in his deep voice.

"I was talking to Carol," Jim Stacey admitted honestly. "Frankly, Centaur, she does not want to be under obligations!"

Centaur King stared in the darkness, and a heavy feeling seemed to envelop him. Then he straightened his shoulders and took a deep seat in the saddle.

"I'll see you to-morrow," he said shortly, and walked his horse out of the yard.

"High-spirited hombre," the sheriff remarked to Stacey. "I reckon we made a mistake, Jim. That money business could have waited, and it didn't do the hoss tamer any good!"

# CHAPTER SEVENTEEN
## MURDER AT MIDNIGHT

Pegasus Bronte busied himself about the camp after Centaur King had disappeared around the bend of the road leading to town. Fresh water for the horses, wood for the morning fire; all the little chores necessary to clean living.

The boy walked to the rear of the Conestoga wagon and gazed thoughtfully at his bunk. He knew that he would sleep soundly after his sketchy slumber of the night before, and Peg turned to study the grove of cottonwoods. Then he nodded his head and stripped his blankets from the bunk. He would sleep in the open just in case.

After spreading a heavy tarpaulin on the ground in a nest of trees just large enough for his bed, Peg Bronte arranged his sleeping quarters and returned to the wagon. There was just enough light left to help locate objects when the boy climbed into the wagon and grinned a bit sheepishly as he stuffed pillows and clothing under the covers in Centaur King's bunk. He laid an old hat on the pillow and stood back to survey his work.

Now it looked like a man sleeping in the bunk,

245

and Peg took the thirty rifle and his duelling pistol. Not that he was afraid, he told himself, but a man would have more chance to put up a fight if he had a bit of warning.

In furtherance of his plan, the boy changed the horses on their picket lines and moved them down closer to his bed. They would be almost as good as watch-dogs in the event that prowlers visited the camp, but Peg Bronte did not admit even to himself that he was thinking about Colt Johnson.

It was after dark when he finished his preparations for the long night. The horses had settled down to grazing, and it would be an hour or so before the moon rose above the Sandias. A peculiar feeling of restlessness plagued Peg Bronte, and he walked slowly toward the golden stallion for companionship.

Golden whickered softly and nuzzled the boy gently. Peg Bronte caressed the smooth shoulders and arching neck. He talked in a low voice, much in the same way he talked to little Madeline. Telling the golden palomino of his hopes and fears, and ridding himself of that repression which comes from keeping things locked up inside.

Velvety darkness settled over the camp, and Peg Bronte shrugged his shoulders. He and Centaur King had been soaked in the rain, and now was a good time for a bath. There was a deep place in the creek where he got water for the horses, and Peg Bronte slipped through the trees and undressed on the sloping bank.

The water was just cold enough to be invigorating, and after swimming vigorously for a time, the boy dried himself on a huck towel and resumed his clothing. He felt better after his swim, and Pegasus returned to camp and sat on his bed. After a while he began to yawn, and pulling off his boots, the boy crawled between his blankets.

The duelling pistol was under his pillow, with the thirty rifle close to his hand alongside the blankets. He could see the top of the wagon outlined against the sky, and the sounds of the horses cropping the grass was soothing. Then Peg Bronte closed his eyes and was asleep almost instantly.

The hours passed, and once the boy stirred restlessly when one of the horses whinnied. Peg Bronte's right hand touched the pistol under his pillow, but he did not arouse himself to wakefulness.

Now the horses had returned to their feeding, and the pale sickle moon topped the low mountains to cast a sickly half-light over the sleeping camp. A dark figure moved slightly away from the shadows down on the road near the gate. Then the skulking figure merged with the shadows and moved toward the wagon without making the slightest sound.

Even the horses down near the grove of cottonwoods were not disturbed again after that first warning. But the menacing figure could see the horses, and the tall slender man kept the wagon between himself and the animals as he moved toward the wagon in a crouch.

Now the man was near the back of the wagon, and a vagrant moonbeam glittered on the naked six-shooter in his right hand. For a long moment the skulker stood perfectly still, staring at the bunk inside the wagon. He could make out the form of a sleeper under the blankets, and the six-shooter rose slowly and steadied.

Two bellowing explosions shattered the stillness of the night as the heavy six-shooter roared and kicked up in the killer's hand. The horses snorted and ran to the ends of their ropes, and Peg Bronte gasped and came up out of his blankets with the pistol in his hand.

The boy trembled from shock and reaction as he tried to get his bearings. He could see the wagon a hundred yards away and he strained his eyes to detect some movement. He knew that he must have slept several hours, because now the sickle moon was riding high and shedding a stronger light.

Peg Bronte crouched on his blankets as he shed the numbing shackles of sleep. Then he stuck the pistol down in the band of his riding breeches and reached for the thirty gun. Those shots had come from near the wagon, and the range was too great for pistol shooting.

Perspiration bathed the boy as he moved slowly and got behind a tree. He was just lining his sights on the wagon when a six-shooter roared again from near the rear of the wagon. An answering shot came from the trail leading to the gate, and then the two guns cracked in unison.

Peg Bronte held his fire because he saw nothing to shoot at, and because Centaur King had taught him never to shoot blindly. It might be the horse tamer returning from town, or one of Jim Stacey's men.

The shooting stopped and Peg Bronte held his post and strained his eyes for some sign of movement. The minutes dragged along leadenly, and then Pegasus heard the thud of hooves in the near distance. The sounds grew fainter and died away, and then Peg Bronte slipped from tree to tree as he made his way toward the ghostly outlines of the big wagon.

The trees cast a long shadow almost up to the wagon, and the boy crept across the clearing on his belly. He reached the wagon, wriggled underneath, and made his way to the back. He wondered who the second man was, knowing that he must be somewhere between the wagon and the gate.

Peg Bronte hugged the ground under the wagon and stared down the little hill leading to the gate.

A horse whinnied from down on the road, and Peg cocked his head to listen. That was not Major Domo. The black stallion always whistled shrilly when returning to camp, and a man would be a fool to show himself in the moonlight.

The boy pulled his dinky hat low over his eyes to cover the whiteness of his face which would stand out in the surrounding darkness. Then he heard a low muffled groan off to the right, and not more than thirty yards away. Peg Bronte placed the sound in a clump of brush, and covered the clump with his rifle. Again he heard a groan as though someone were in pain.

Peg Bronte was about to call out when he remembered what Centaur King had told him about outlaws. They were deadly as long as they could hold a gun, and the groan might be a trick to lure him into the open. Then the boy saw a movement in the brush, and his finger tightened on the trigger of the rifle.

"Kid!" a voice called weakly. "Peg Bronte!"

The boy jerked when he heard his name called. The voice sounded vaguely familiar, and after a pause, he answered cautiously.

"Yeah; who's calling?"

"Don't shoot, Kid!" the voice answered quickly. "It's Sam Bailey, and I'm hit bad!"

"Come out in the clear!" Peg answered sharply. "What in time are you doing down here at this time of night?"

The shadow moved and took form as a big man crawled from the brush. Peg Bronte followed the movements with his gun, and he saw Sam Bailey stop moving and settled down on the ground in the moonlight. The boy called sharply, and when he received no answer, he stretched to his feet with the rifle still covering the prostrate man.

Now it was becoming clear to Peg Bronte that Sam Bailey had been one of the participants in the duel he had heard, but which he could not see because of the wagon, and the slight grade leading to the grade where Sam Bailey was now lying. Pegasus remembered the retreating thud of hooves, but he was cautious as he moved slowly toward Bailey.

He stopped a few paces from Bailey and watched for sign of movement. But Sam Bailey did not move, and both hands were empty as they stretched out ahead of his shoulders. No sound came from the burly rancher, and Peg Bronte moved closer and touched Bailey's shoulder. The touch aroused the wounded man and he tried to raise his head.

"Help me, Kid," Bailey muttered drowsily. "I thought . . . he . . . killed you in . . . the . . . wagon!" Understanding flooded across Peg Bronte's mind at the halting, whispered words. Then his hunch had been right, and someone had tried to kill him, mistaking the dummy in Centaur

King's bunk. That someone could be no one but Colt Johnson, and Peg Bronte laid his rifle aside and went to his knees beside Bailey.

"Where you hit, Mister Bailey?" Pegasus asked gently. "And was it . . . Colt Johnson?"

"It was Johnson," the wounded man answered weakly. "Got me in the left leg, and high in the left breast!"

"Dogies!" Peg Bronte ejaculated. "That's exactly the way he got Marshal Crag Tinsley. Now I'll help you roll over while I tie a tight string on your leg the way Centaur did 'er for the marshal!"

As Sam Bailey tried to turn, the boy got behind him and pushed with all his strength. Bailey rolled over, breathing heavily, and Peg Bronte took the bandanna from the cattleman's throat. He rolled it swiftly, passed it under the wounded leg, and made a tight tourniquet to stop the bleeding.

The effort of turning had used up all of Sam Bailey's waning strength, and he sighed and closed his eyes. Pegasus shuddered when he saw the crimson stain on the cattleman's shirt, but he unbuttoned the garment and used his own handkerchief for a compress.

"Got to get him to a doctor," Peg Bronte muttered. "And I can't move him by myself!"

Running back to the wagon, the boy got a pan and clean rags, filled the pan with water, and returned to Bailey. He washed the chest wound and fashioned a cloth plug which he pushed into the bullet hole, and then he again applied a compress and made an awkward bandage.

"I've got to harness the team," Pegasus muttered. "I gotta get old Sam to town before he bleeds out, but how in time am I goin' to drag him in the wagon?"

After doing all he could for the unconscious man, Peg Bronte ran to the grove and brought up the bay team. The golden stallion whinnied with excitement as the boy harnessed the team. Then Pegasus had to move Golden close to the wagon, and he spanned in the team of bays and fastened the tugs and neck-yoke.

"Saved my life, that's what he did," Pegasus told himself fiercely. "I'll drive the wagon close and drag him in if I bust a hame strap!"

He mounted the driver's seat and turned the big wagon expertly. Then he drove close to Sam Bailey and set his brakes. He was kneeling beside the wounded man when one of the bay horses whinnied shrilly.

Peg Bronte jumped from the wagon, scooped up his rifle, and faced the gate with the weapon ready for a shot. If Colt Johnson was coming back to finish what he had started, he'd meet a warm reception before the killer could get close enough for pistol range. Then Peg Bronte heard an answering whinny, and he recognized the shrill call of the black stallion. Centaur King was coming back home!

"Centaur!" the boy yelled. "Come a running!"

Centaur King heard the cry, and he abandoned his caution. He nudged Major Domo with a heel, and the stallion leaped into a gallop. King was going to stop to open the gate, but the stallion did not hesitate. Then King saw that the gate was open, and he raced up the slope to the wagon.

Instantly the horse tamer saw that the wagon had been moved, and then he saw the team spanned in. He also saw Pegasus Bronte standing guard over a fallen man, rifle in hands, and King slid to a stop and made a running dismount.

"What happened?" he asked tersely. "And who's the victim?"

"Sam Bailey," Pegasus answered. "We got to get him to the doctor fast, Centaur. Colt Johnson sneaked down here and tried to kill me, but I had moved by bed down in the trees. I don't know how old Sam got down this way, but him and that killer fought a gun-smoke duel. Johnson got Sam Bailey the same way he got Crag Tinsley!"

Centaur King was examining the wounded man as Pegasus made his staccato explanation. King eased the tourniquet off for a time, tightened it again, and tightened the chest bandage. Then he went to the wagon to prepare a bed on the floor. He stopped with his nostrils flaring when he saw the piled blankets in his bunk.

Crawling into the wagon, the horse tamer stared at the dummy in his bed. His finger poked two bullet holes where Colt Johnson had fired at which he had thought was the body of Pegasus Bronte.

Centaur King stared and rubbed his chin gently. His black beard was a two-day stubble, and the horse tamer's eyes burned with a terrible light of repressed anger. He sucked in a deep breath, touched the gun on his right leg, and then picked up the blankets. After making a bed on the floor of the wagon, King climbed out and went back to the wounded man.

"We'll do the best we can, Peg," he told the boy. "I'll take his shoulders where he's the heaviest, and you get his boots."

"He got this fighting for me," Peg Bronte whispered. "After him starting that stampede like he did!"

"Sorry about stampede," a hoarse voice murmured weakly.

Centaur King knelt beside the cattleman. "How'd you know, Sam?" he asked gently. "That Peg was down here alone?"

"Saw you ride into town," Bailey whispered. "Then I thought I saw Colt Johnson, but I wasn't sure. I owed you and the button something for what I did, so I rode on down here. Did you see Johnson?" he asked.

"No, but I'll hunt him down now!" King

promised sternly. "He knew I was at the marshal's house; knew Peg was down here alone. He thinks he's killed Pegasus, but you scared him off before he could make sure!"

"I thought Peg was done," Bailey whispered. "I saw Johnson shoot twice into the wagon. I lost my head and blazed away, and there I was sky-lined again the moon!"

"Thanks, pard," Centaur King said gratefully. "You've more than evened up your score, and Peg and me will see that you get to old Doc Snyder's place. Steady now, we're going to pick you up and stow you in the wagon."

Sam Bailey set his teeth when King slid his strong hands under the wounded man's shoulders. He had felt those muscles once before, but this was different. Centaur King nodded at Pegasus and straightened his legs. He lifted Sam Bailey's bulk easily, walked to the wagon with Peg Bronte carrying the heavy legs, and then Sam Bailey sighed as he was laid on the blankets.

"You take the ribbons and do the driving, Peg," King told the boy. "I'll stay here with Sam until we get closer to town. Then I'll ride Major Domo ahead and have the doctor ready by the time you get there. Don't run the horses; it might hurt Sam and start him to bleeding again!"

"Like you said, Centaur," Pegasus agreed, and he climbed to the driver's seat.

Peg Bronte laid the rifle on the seat beside

him, picked up the reins, and started the team. King had fastened Major Domo to the tail-gate, and now he sat beside the wounded man in the wagon.

"We won't forget what you did to-night, Sam," he told the cattleman, but Sam Bailey had again lapsed into unconsciousness.

Centaur King made sure the chest bandage had not slipped, released the tourniquet for a while, and tightened it again. He wondered if Colt Johnson was lurking in the brush, and then the horse tamer shrugged. He remembered that Colt Johnson had promised to give warning before he struck, and for some unknown reason, Centaur King believed the killer.

Not that he would take Johnson's word for anything else, but a gun-fighter had a peculiar code of ethics. Especially where his skill was concerned, and Colt Johnson had boasted that he was fast with his killer gun. He was also inordinately vain.

Crag Tinsley and Peg Bronte were different. The marshal had sent Johnson to prison, and Peg Bronte had taken at him from the dark. He had promised to get the marshal, and he had settled with the brash hairpin. But with Centaur King, the killer had passed his word to give King an even break, and King smiled coldly as he stared from the wagon.

It was about two miles to Lanthrope when King

jumped from the wagon and untied Major Domo. He mounted up, rode ahead, and spoke to Peg Bronte.

"I'll ride ahead and have everything ready, Pegasus. Take it easy so as not to jolt Sam. He's passed out again, but I'm sure he will be all right."

"Watch yourself, Centaur!" the boy warned. "Colt Johnson won't sleep until he whittles your notch, or you smoke him down one!"

Centaur King waved his hand and sent Major Domo ahead in a dead run. He left the wagon rapidly behind, and gradually the street lights of Lanthrope grew brighter. Ten minutes later he slid to a stop in front of Doctor Snyder's house, latched the stallion to a picket, and hammered on the front door.

"Who's there?" a rasping voice demanded. "At this ungodly hour of the night?"

"Centaur King, Doc!" the horse tamer answered. "Sam Bailey has been shot, and Pegasus is bringing him in the wagon. Get into your clothes and shake a leg!"

# CHAPTER EIGHTEEN
## THE GO-AHEAD

Doc Snyder opened the front door and told Centaur King to come in and to scrub his hands. King could hear the old Medico muttering as he dressed, and then Snyder came to scrub his hands and to ask questions.

"Who's the victim this time, and how bad is he shot?"

"It's Sam Bailey, Doc," King answered. "He's shot almost the same way and in the same places as Crag Tinsley, and the same man shot Bailey."

"You'll have to help me," the doctor grunted. "Colt Johnson can wait until we patch up Bailey," and he glared at King.

"I was going right on out," King said hesitantly. "You see, Doc, Johnson thought he had killed Pegasus, and Bailey took up the fight. I was up at Tinsley's, but I got back there to help Peg get Bailey into the wagon."

"Yeah, well, Colt Johnson can still wait," the doctor grunted, and he raised his head to listen. "Yonder comes your wagon, so we better get out there."

Sam Bailey was unconscious when they carried him into the doctor's office. King told Pegasus

259

to go up to the Tinsley place and notify Sheriff Ben Clay. Doc Snyder was examining Bailey's wounds, and he asked King to help him strip the wounded man's shirts.

"You know what to do with those surgical sponges," the old Medico growled. "We'll probe that slug out of his leg first, and then take care of him up above."

"Yes, Suh," King answered respectfully.

"Hmm," Snyder grunted. "You could be a gentleman if you chose, King. Probe!"

"Yes, Suh!" King murmured, and passed the probe.

With the leg wound bandaged, Sam Bailey showed signs of returning consciousness. The doctor filled a hypodermic syringe and gave the wounded man an injection, and then he started to work on the chest wound.

"This Colt Johnson," the doctor said, as he worked. "He always shoots a bit high, King. When you and him smoke it out, you'll still have a chance of survival."

"A man can't live forever," King answered gruffly.

"Won't she talk to you yet?" the doctor asked, without looking up.

"No," King answered, and made no attempt at evasion. "So Peg and me will be rolling westward as soon as I finish a little business here."

"Yeah, well, good luck, horse tamer," Doc

Snyder said dryly. "But you'll be back again."

Centaur King did not answer, and when the work was finished, he washed thoroughly and put on his coat. He could hear low voices talking outside, and Sheriff Clay called to King as he stepped through the door.

"Over here, Centaur. How's Sam making it?"

"He will make the grade," King answered confidently. "Howdy, Jim."

Dapper Jim Stacey shook his head and came close to King. "Better drive your wagon back under the cottonwoods where you and Peg camped before," he suggested. "The sheriff and I are riding with you."

King turned to Peg Bronte and told the boy to drive the team back to their original camp site. Peg frowned and fingered the pistol in his belt.

"Can I go along, Centaur?" he asked wistfully.

"You stay and guard the wagon," King answered brusquely, and his face was set in hard lines.

"Like you said, but take care of yourself, pard," Peg answered manfully. "If I was you I'd hit saddle and get long gone!"

King turned quickly to stare at the boy, and he followed Peg's glance up the street. Carol Tinsley was riding toward them, and Centaur King walked swiftly to his horse. He mounted and was about to leave, when Carol called to him.

"Please wait a minute, Centaur!"

King reined about and rode to meet the girl. It lacked an hour until sun-up and Jim Stacey and the sheriff had gone to saddle their horses.

"I heard, Centaur," the girl said shakily. "Colt Johnson tried to kill Pegasus, and he wounded Sam Bailey!"

"That's right," King agreed. "But he made me a promise like you know!"

"You mean you are going to face him for a shoot-out?" the girl asked in a whisper.

"That's right," King admitted. "Might as well get it over with."

Carol shuddered and reached for King's hand. She clung to the hand, but Centaur King refused to meet her eyes.

"You won't give it up if I ask you?" she pleaded.

King slowly shook his head. "That's right," he said. "He tried to kill Pegasus, and he means to kill me." Then he smiled at the girl and returned the pressure of her fingers. "Don't worry, Carol," he said quietly. "I have a feeling, and I can promise you that everything will come out right!"

Carol Tinsley leaned closer and offered her lips. Centaur King leaned over and kissed her full on the lips.

"I'll be back," he said slowly. "I'll be seeing you!"

He wheeled his horse and rode to meet Jim Stacey and the sheriff as they cantered out of the sales ring. Peg Bronte waved his hand at King, and then climbed into the driver's seat. He was staking the horses out when Carol rode under the trees and dismounted.

"Come here, Peg," she called to the boy.

Peg Bronte frowned and came reluctantly. "What you want?" he asked ungraciously.

"This," Carol said, and she took him in her arms. "If anything had happened to you to-night, Centaur and I would never have gotten over it," she whispered, and kissed the boy's cheek.

Peg Bronte listened and quivered like a high-strung horse. "You mean, you'd have cared?" he asked slowly.

"Oh, Peg," Carol sobbed. "You have been so loyal and so brave. I love you most as much as I do . . ."

"You mean . . . Centaur?"

"That's just what I mean," Carol answered tremulously. "And now he might not return!"

"Gwan!" Pegasus snorted. "Centaur has that outlaw faded, and he can call his shots. Now you looky here, Miss Carol," he continued fiercely. "When Centaur comes back, don't go hiding him about killing another hombre who needs killin'! You hear me?"

"I hear you, Peg," the girl murmured. "I won't even mention it, but I'm afraid!"

"Shuckins, Ma'am," Peg blurted. "You don't have to be afraid for Centaur. He'll dot that owl-hooter's squinchy eyes and leave him lay for the buzzards!"

"I'll wait here with you if you don't mind," Carol said slowly.

"Proud to have you, Miss Carol," Pegasus answered with enthusiasm. "I done made up my sleep, and come daylight, I'll cook us up a mess of hot vittles!"

"They headed north," Carol said thoughtfully. "That means only one thing, Peg. They are riding back to Painted Cave!"

Centaur King was in the lead as the three men rode through the scrub-oak toward the low foothills. He felt no emotion as the cool wind blew in his face, and his voice was low and steady when he spoke to Sheriff Clay.

"I'm asking a favour, Sheriff."

"Nothing doing," Ben Clay answered sternly. "We'll surround that killer and give him a chance to surrender. He might kill you in a shoot-out!"

"Then we'll never take him," King said quietly. "He made me a promise, and I'm sure he will keep it!"

"Don't do it, Centaur," Jim Stacey added his protest. "You've seen what he did to Crag and to Sam Bailey!"

"And the sheriff saw what I did to Pete Powers," King retorted. "Now we might as well get this straight. Either I meet Johnson for an even break, or I'm riding back to town!"

The sun came up as he finished speaking, and Sheriff Clay stared intently at the horse tamer's stern face. The three-day stubble of black beard added a fierceness to King's appearance, and the sheriff turned to look at Jim Stacey.

"Better let him have his way, Ben," the auctioneer advised. "Otherwise he will do like he said, and then all he will be is a target for that killer."

"I don't like it none, but have it your way," the sheriff agreed glumly. "What makes you think he's back in Painted Cave?" he asked King.

"It's just a hunch," King admitted. "Perhaps it has something to do with a killer going back to the scene of his crime. In this case, Painted Cave is where he challenged me, and he knows a thousand men are looking for him outside.

"Look to your gun, King," Clay warned grimly. "You won't get but one chance, and mebbe not that!"

King nodded and drew his six-shooter. He checked the loads, tried the balance, and holstered the gun deep in his holster. Then he nodded and touched the black stallion with a heel.

He could hear Jim Stacey and the sheriff talking behind him as they entered the foothills and began the gradual climb. But King did not want to talk, and he was forming a mental picture of the lean, buck-toothed killer. When he thought of the attempt on Pegasus Bronte in the wagon, King's blood began to hum through his veins.

His was the perfect health of the outdoors man who neither drank nor smoked. Peg Bronte had confidence in him, and Carol Tinsley had wished him good luck. The sun climbed in the sky, and when King glanced at his watch, the hour was seven. He glanced at the cluster known as Whispering Rocks, and waited for Jim Stacey and the sheriff to come up.

"I'm going around, King," the sheriff said quietly, with his head turned away from the ring of rocks. "If he gets you, I'm going in the back way after him, while Jim guards this lower trail!"

"I'll be seeing you, Sheriff," King answered confidently.

"I hope so," Clay grunted. "*Hasta la vista!*"

Stacey watched King as the sheriff rode away to climb the round-about trail behind the cave high up on the hill. Centaur King dismounted and tied his horse with trailing reins. Then he loosed his gun in the holster, walked to the cluster of rocks, and spoke clearly.

"I am here, Johnson. Centaur King speaking!"

"I saw you coming," the snarling answer came through the rocks. "So you didn't pack the sand to come alone!"

"I'll come alone, up the path like I did before," King answered. "I'll meet you on that little shelf where I took the baby. You give the go-ahead!"

"That thick-headed shur'ff thinks he has me boxed up," Johnson sneered. "I set off a charge of black powder and closed up that back way in. That dude with you hasn't a rifle, so it's still between you and me!"

"Yeah," King agreed. "Are you still going to rattle before you strike?"

"I said I'd give you an even break, didn't I?" the outlaw snarled. "I got you faded, and we both know it. Start walking up the trail, and I'll start coming down!"

"I should have snuck up there and hid," Jim Stacey whispered, but Centaur King smiled.

"Colt Johnson would have seen you," he answered, and then he tightened the Stetson on his black head.

He didn't say good-bye to Stacey; just started up the trail with both hands swinging loosely at his sides. Halfway up, King saw the lathy outlaw coming toward him, and Johnson was also empty-handed.

Centaur King watched the killer with a touch of admiration. Colt Johnson knew that escape was impossible, and that death was certain if he was captured. But the outlaw showed no fear, and Centaur King realized that Johnson had it all figured. The killer had nothing to lose, and he was superbly confident of his own abilities.

Now the two men were getting closer; close

enough for either of them to risk a shot. But neither hesitated nor slowed up, and they met on the flat little shelf where King had paid the money, and had taken little Madeline by the hand.

They stopped ten paces apart and studied each other. Colt Johnson's face was covered with a stubble of red beard, but Centaur King looked equally as fierce with his black stubble. Johnson wore his twin guns thonged low on his lean thighs, while King wore the gun the sheriff had given him.

"I see you are still wearing Al's hog-leg," Johnson commented.

"That's right," King agreed. "I tried it out, and it shoots straight."

"You're a dead man, but you don't know it yet," Johnson sneered.

"I'm no deader'n Peg Bronte," King answered quietly, and he smiled when he saw the outlaw jerk.

"So you was back to your camp," Johnson said. "Did you find another ringy gent who went on the prod and brought me smoke?"

"That's why I was a bit late," King answered with a nod. "I brought Sam Bailey to town and helped the doctor patch him up. Doc Snyder says to tell you you are throwing your shots off, and placing 'em high!"

His answer was a snarling curse as Colt

Johnson went into a crouch. "That salty hairpin is dead!" the outlaw boasted.

"Never touched him," King contradicted. "But you tried to kill him, so give the go-ahead whenever you're ready!"

"You've got sand, I'll give you that," the killer admitted grudgingly. "I could drop my hat, or you could drop yours."

"One of us might grab an edge," King replied.

"You start making your pass, and I'll play what I catch on the draw," Johnson suggested eagerly, and both hands shadowed the brace of guns in his holsters.

"You getting shaky?" King taunted, knowing that anger slows up the muscles.

"Draw!" Johnson blurted, and his greenish eyes were pin-points of flame between slitted lids. "Draw before I let you have it!"

"Hold it!" Centaur King said sternly, and his voice was edgy. "You say you're not shaky. Looky yonder at that lizard between us. There's a bug not far from the lizard. Pretty soon he will move closer. Then it will shove up and down on its front legs. You've watched 'em many's the time."

"Yeah, so what?" Johnson snarled, but his eyes were watching the lizard.

"So then the lizard will get in position," King continued. "All of a sudden it will leap forward, lick out its tongue, and the bug will disappear.

When the lizard makes that last leap . . . ?"

"That's the go-ahead!" Johnson agreed in a hoarse whisper.

Both men crouched forward with hands above their holstered guns. Both were staring intently at the lizard, which suddenly moved forward a fraction. Neither man moved a hand. Both stared at the reptile, and the helpless bug which seemed incapable of movement.

Centaur King was steady and poised as he watched the lizard intently, but without blinking his eyes. He had practised the art of concentration; had held his hand steady for many a snapping horse.

Colt Johnson was like a statue as he held his crouch . . . and both taloned hands. His hat was at the back of his balding head, and the outlaw was breathing through his long buck teeth, making a little whistling sound.

The lizard moved up again and poised. Then it began the little "push-up" which always precedes a dart for the prey, licking out its long tongue at the same instant.

Colt Johnson struck for his two guns with the speed of long practice. Centaur King dropped his hand and lurched his shoulder for the draw. His six-shooter leaped clear of leather and belched yellow flame with a thunderous roar.

Colt Johnson had both guns in his hands when his left leg buckled beneath him. He triggered with both hands as he was falling, and the twin slugs whistled over King's head.

Colt Johnson went down and dropped his left-hand gun. He started to raise the right when Centaur King squeezed off his second shot, and Johnson was battered to the ground on his back as the slug struck him in the left breast.

Centaur King waited with no expression on his stern set face. When Johnson did not move, King turned the smoking gun in his hand, ejected the spent shells with the ejector rod, and thumbed fresh cartridges through the loading gate.

He seated the smoke-grimed weapon in his holster, and turned to meet Dapper Jim Stacey who was legging it up the path at a dead run.

"You got him, Centaur," the auctioneer shouted. "Is he dead?"

"Naw," King growled low in his throat. "He's got the same thing he gave both Crag and Bailey."

"Why didn't you kill him?" Stacey asked harshly.

Centaur King moved quickly and picked up the guns Colt Johnson had dropped. Johnson sat up weakly, swaying back and forth. He listened as King answered the auctioneer.

"Because I had him faded, and I never bet on a sure thing," King answered quietly.

"But how did you know you had him beat?" Stacey questioned.

"This is why," King explained, pointing to the

two captured guns. "You know something about co-ordination, Jim. Johnson had to think about *two* guns and as many hands and arms, while I concentrated upon one. That little difference made all the difference in the world between him and me!"

"I'm bleeding out," Johnson whispered weakly. "I'll never live to get back to town!"

"Oh, yes you will," King contradicted. "Either way this went, there was work for old Doc Snyder. He's coming up the trail now with his little black bag, and this is one job I won't help him with!"

"What's that?" the old Medico asked sharply. "You'll take off your coat and roll up your sleeves, Centaur King. Or I'll come apart and do you a meanness you won't get over in time to attend Colt Johnson's trial!"

Centaur King sighed and obeyed meekly. The outlaw sighed and lost consciousness, and Doc Snyder laid out his tools.

"Sponge!" he barked at King. "Probe!"

"Yes, Suh," King murmured. "Like you said, Doc!"

272

# CHAPTER NINETEEN
## WANTED

Colt Johnson was a sick man when Doc Snyder finished his work. The outlaw was weak and shaky from nausea and the loss of blood, and was barely conscious of what went on around him.

Centaur King washed at a little rill which trickled down from a clear spring in the rocks. Now the fierce light of battle had faded from the horse tamer's dark eyes, and the edgy raspiness had left his voice when he spoke softly to Dapper Jim Stacey.

"I'm going up to the cave for a look around, Jim. You want to come along?"

Jim Stacey had wanted to go to the cave while the two men were working on Johnson, but he had sensed that King had earned the right of discovery. Now he nodded eagerly and fell in beside King. They climbed the trail leisurely, and as they paused in the cave entrance, a low whinny greeted them.

"That will be Crag Tinsley's strawberry roan," Stacey said positively. "The marshal will be mighty glad to get his horse back again."

King was peering into the big cave, and gradually his eyes became accustomed to the semi-gloom. He walked inside and stopped to study a rude fire-place of rocks where the outlaw had done his camp-cooking.

Jim Stacey called and pointed to some rude paintings on the sandstone walls, explaining that they were the work of Indians before the coming of Cortez. A small stream trickled through the cave about halfway back, and the horse whinnied again.

King walked up to the stout animal and spoke softly. His hands petted the muscled flanks and arching neck. The horse was saddled and ready for a long ride. A bedroll rode behind the saddle, and beneath the bed was a pair of bulging saddle-bags.

Centaur King reached for the saddle-bags with an eager light of anticipation in his eyes. Jim Stacey watched in silence, but he knew what King expected to find. The horse tamer carried the bags to the light, opened them carefully, and started to reach inside. Then he jerked back his hand with a little grunt of surprise.

"*Vinegarone!*" Jim Stacey shouted. "Careful, King; that varmint is a whip scorpion."

But Centaur King had seen the long venomous insect first. He turned the saddle-bag over and emptied it, killing the vicious scorpion with the heel of one boot when it fell wriggling on the sandstone floor.

"He had an ace-in-the-hole!" Stacey whispered.

"He knew you would come up here to search his bags if you won the shoot-out. He put that scorpion in the bag just in case he lost!"

Centaur King shrugged and picked up the canvas sack he had given to Colt Johnson. It contained the ransom money he had paid for the return of little Madeline, and there was also a crumpled note. King smoothed out the cheap paper and read the message.

"It's from Al Johnson," he told Stacey. "It tells Colt Johnson that his brother and Pete Powers were going to rob the Stanhope bank, and it must have been left here in the cave."

"Inside the cave!" a booming voice shouted. "Are you and Jim in there, King?"

Centaur King recognized the sheriff's voice, and he called an answer. Ben Clay puffed up the steep trail and stared at the sack of money. Then he saw the note in King's hand, and reaching for it, he read it slowly.

"They will stretch Colt Johnson's scrawny neck," the sheriff said quietly, and then he studied King's face with a quizzical expression in his eyes.

"Why didn't you kill that outlaw, King?" he asked.

"I'm not a killer," King answered with a quiet dignity. "I only shot in self-defence and now I won't have his death on my conscience!"

"His death wouldn't make me lose any sleep,"

Clay said gruffly. "He will be tried in my county where he committed his crimes!"

"He didn't commit murder," King reminded the peace officer.

"That's right," Clay agreed reluctantly. "But he'll get life imprisonment. Now if you had lowered your sights just an inch . . . ?"

"If Johnson had lowered his sights just an inch, both Crag Tinsley and Sam Bailey would be dead now," King answered quietly. "He set the pattern, and I just followed it!"

"We'll have to use the marshal's horse to take Johnson back to town," the sheriff changed the subject, and went back to lead out the strawberry roan.

Doc Snyder was smoking a twisted quirly when the three men came down the path leading the marshal's horse. The old Medico dropped his cigarette and set his boot on the spark. He said he had given his patient something to dull the pain, and Colt Johnson did not awake when they raised him to the saddle and made him secure.

"We can manage, Centaur," Jim Stacey said to King. "You'll want to get back to town, and we won't feel hard toward you if you light a shuck now."

"Thanks, feller," King answered gratefully. "Pegasus will be a mite worried, so I'll be getting back there."

"Peg won't be the only one waiting to hear,"

276

Doc Snyder said dryly. "But on your way, horse tamer. You'd make a good Medico if you set your mind to it!"

"I don't like blood," King said with a smile, and he was already legging it toward his black stallion. He mounted Major Domo and whirled the big horse, and then he left the three men and their prisoner with a little wave of his hand.

Major Domo sensed the eagerness of his master to get back to town, and the black stallion struck out down the back trail with a smooth lope which ate up the miles. They reached the end of the street in Lanthrope at high noon, and Centaur King passed the auction ring and rode directly to the big Conestoga wagon. Peg Bronte came running to meet him, shouting a welcome.

"Howdy, Centaur. Glad you're back again. Long time no see!"

"Gwan!" King growled as he swung to the ground. "I haven't been gone but five-six hours!"

"Did you get that side-winder?" Peg Bronte demanded eagerly. "Did you drill him plumb centre?"

"Look, pard," King answered quietly. "I'm not a cold killer, and you know it."

The boy lowered his eyes and studied the smoke-grimed gun. His voice was accusing when he stared at King's calm face.

"You throwed off yore shot, Centaur! You beat

that owl-hooter to the draw, and then you only winged him!"

"Yeah," King agreed. "Like you said, Pegasus. But I've better news than that. The money I paid Colt Johnson was standing between Carol and me, and I recovered every dollar of the ransom. Now neither she nor Crag will feel under any obligations!"

"Shh!" Pegasus warned softly, and he shook his head and pointed to the wagon when King stared at him. Then Peg pointed to the driver's seat, and turning his back, he went to the fire to look after his pots and pans.

Centaur King removed his Stetson and faced the front of the wagon. He dropped his bridle reins to the ground to make a ground-hitch, and then he saw his face in a little mirror hanging at the back of the wagon.

King grinned as he passed a long-fingered hand over the stubble of black beard. It certainly changed his appearance, and for a moment he hesitated. Then he took a deep breath and started toward the front of the wagon.

Carol Tinsley looked up, and her eyes were brimming with unshed tears. Without speaking, she reached out her hands. Centaur King took them eagerly and drew the girl closer.

"I've come back, Carol," he said gently, and his deep vibrant voice was like a caress. "Like I told you I would!"

Carol Tinsley nodded and hid her face against his shoulder. She did not trust herself to speak, and King's hands patted her shoulders as he revelled in the thrill of her nearness.

"I recovered the ransom money," he said after a silence.

"Yes, I heard," Carol whispered. "Can you forgive me for being so ungrateful?"

"I know how you felt," King consoled her. "And Crag will get his horse back."

"Crag will be glad," Carol murmured, and then she raised her head and smiled as she stared at his stubble of beard. "You do need a shave, Centaur," she reproved gently. "I'll help Pegasus with the food, while you make yourself presentable."

Centaur King turned to see Pegasus watching him. His arms fell away from the girl, and he walked to the back of the wagon. Peg Bronte brought hot water and filled a basin, and King shucked his coat and stripped off his linen shirt.

"Look at them muscles," Pegasus said admiringly, as he pointed to the long powerful muscles in King's shoulders and arms. "He's the strongest hombre in these parts, Carol!"

Carol Tinsley looked and nodded her curly head. Centaur King reproved Pegasus sternly.

"Save your breath to cool your broth, young fellow! And you might have told me there was a lady present!"

"Me and Carol had a nice long visit," Peg Bronte boasted.

"Carol and I," King corrected.

"But not as long as me and Carol did," Pegasus retorted with a grin.

Centaur King acknowledged defeat with a shrug. He lathered his beard and applied the straight sharp blade, while Peg Bronte watched with envy.

"I'll soon be shaving myself," he said hopefully, and passed his hand over his smooth cheeks.

"Yeah, you're growing," King admitted slowly. "It won't be long now before you will be crowding me for honours."

"I won't ever crowd you, Centaur," the boy said soberly. "But I am learning a lot of things."

"You're the best camp cook I ever ate after," King praised, as he rinsed his face.

"There's more important things than cooking," Pegasus pouted. "There's responsibility, for an instance, and thinking about other folks besides yourself!"

Centaur King stopped washing and stared at the boy. Peg Bronte was digging a hole with the toe of one boot, and Carol Tinsley was placing dishes on the tail-gate of the wagon.

"I'll say you are learning, pardner," King answered slowly. "And seems to me as though you had a mighty good teacher!"

"Me and Carol did a mess of talking," Peg growled. "I like her a heap, Centaur!"

"You want to be careful, hoss tamer," King said with a smile. "There might be someone around here who would be getting jealous of you!"

Carol Tinsley busied herself near the fire and pretended not to hear. Centaur King winked at Pegasus and climbed into the wagon to get clean clothes. When he came back to the fire, he wore his best suit, a clean white shirt and tie, and polished hand-made boots.

"I'm hungry," King said, as he sniffed the savoury odours rising from the steaming pots. "If I don't smell roast pork, you can trade me in for a razor-back hog!"

"Carol fixed that pork roast," Pegasus answered with a grin. "She wanted to know what you liked best, and I gave her the low-down."

"You mean sweet potato pie and shoe-string potatoes?" King whispered, and he winked at Peg Bronte when Carol flushed with embarrassment.

"Just wait until you sink a fang in that pie," Pegasus said with a nod. "And Centaur, you never saw anything as pretty as those pictures she painted of the horses!"

"You mean you brought them down?" King asked eagerly.

"After dinner," Carol said sternly. "We got out the little table, and dinner will be ready in half a minute. You look mighty handsome again, Mister

King," she said with genuine approval. "You scared me with all those whiskers."

"I thank you, Miss Carol," King bantered happily. "A woman's touch certainly adds something, doesn't it, Peg?" he appealed to the boy.

"I'll tell a man," Peg agreed with enthusiasm. "I wish Carol would travel with us all the time!"

"Peggie!" Carol scolded. "You should think before you say such things!"

"I'm sorry, and don't call me Peggie," the boy muttered.

"Come and get it!" Carol sang out, as she placed the roast on the little table. "You sit at that end, Centaur. You at the other, Pegasus."

"May I seat you?" King asked courteously.

"I'll be up and down," Carol answered happily. "You men be seated and start eating. Don't let the food get cold, or I'll be angry with both of you."

"You heard what the boss said, Centaur," Pegasus said impudently. "Say!" he whispered. "You forgot to strap on your gun!"

"I didn't forget," King said coldly. "I don't need a gun any more."

"I'm glad, Centaur," Carol said gratefully. "I didn't like you near as well when you were wearing that horrid gun."

"The food smells delicious," King said with appreciation.

"Can I wear that outlaw gun now?" Pegasus persisted.

King looked at the boy and tightened his lips. "You cannot," he answered sternly. "In our profession, gun fighting does not fit in with gentling horses."

"You did right well," Pegasus pouted.

"That will do, Peg," King said firmly. "I haven't handled a horse since this trouble started, and you know it. How is Crag?" he asked Carol.

"Believe it or not, but he is sitting propped up today," the girl answered happily. "Now let's eat before the food gets cold."

Pegasus Bronte ate silently, but he was watching the face of Centaur King. Now the horse tamer seemed relaxed and contented, and his eyes were gentle and smiling.

King was eating slowly but with evident relish, and he was watching Carol Tinsley as the girl got up now and then to add some delicacy to the laden table. When the meal was finished, King sighed with satisfaction.

"That's the best meal I've ever eaten," he praised sincerely. "Peg and I will never be satisfied after this with our own cooking. Will we, pard?"

"I'll say we won't," the boy answered soberly. "Ain't there some way we could figger out to take Carol along with us?"

"Peggie," Carol scolded, and her face was rosy with colour. "What in the world are you saying?"

"Remember what I told you, Peg," King added.

"When you grow up, you don't say everything you think."

"I was only saying what you was thinking," Pegasus grumbled.

"That will do, Peg!" King said sternly.

"Well, I like Carol," the boy argued. "Next to you, I like her better than anyone in the world, except Sugar Foots!"

"Thank you, Peg," Carol whispered, and she pressed the boy's hand. "But Centaur is right, and you mustn't think out loud."

"Do you think you could persuade the marshal to get a wagon and take a trip while he is healing up?" King asked the girl.

Carol shook her head sadly. "I'm afraid not," she sighed. "I'd love it for a while, to live in the open, and to paint some pictures here and there."

"Me and Centaur are rolling west soon," Peg interrupted. "You could go along with us, Carol!"

Centaur King coughed and excused himself. Carol showed her embarrassment, and she got up and began to clear the table. Peg helped her with the dishes, and King busied himself about the wagon with this and that. Hanging up his old clothes, mending a bit of leather; anything to keep his mind away from the trend of thought which persisted in his mind since Pegasus had talked so plainly.

Pegasus Bronte finished his chores and stared at King's broad back. Then he squared his shoulders and came to King. He touched the horse tamer on the arm and spoke up manfully.

"I'm saying I'm sorry I spoke with my big mouth wide open, Centaur," he apologized humbly. "We were so glad to see you come a-ridin' back from Painted Cave, and I reckon I just spilled over!"

Centaur King turned swiftly with a happy smile lighting his handsome face. "It's quite all right, Peg," he said quietly. "Here's my hand on it, and we won't say any more about it!"

"Are we going to Stanhope?" Peg asked.

"Yes, in a day or two," King answered.

"I've been practising that double roll on the drum," Peg admitted proudly. "I can do it fine now, and I've been training Gold 'Un to prance at heel!"

Centaur King glanced at Carol to see if the girl had heard. He could tell that she had been listening, and then Pegasus spoke again.

"Carol would come if you'd ask her, pard," the boy whispered. "Me and her both like you, and me and Carol both want you!"

"Mind your manners, Peg," King corrected quietly. "Carol and I both want you!"

"You do?" Peg asked, and leaping into the air he cracked his heels together.

Centaur King sighed and started to turn away. Then he saw Carol watching him, and Centaur King made up his mind.

"Pegasus, you run down to the store and get some butter," he told the boy.

"I got butter this morning," Peg answered.

"I mean apple butter," King said quietly. "And get a box of candy for Sugar Foots!"

"I reckon I know when I'm not wanted," the boy pouted, but he put on his hat and started away.

"But you are wanted, Peg," Carol said softly. "You'll never know just how much you are wanted."

Pegasus smiled then and hurried toward town. Centaur King came slowly toward the girl and studied her soberly. Carol refused to meet his eyes, and King took her left hand.

"Out of the mouths of babes and sucklings," he quoted just above his breath. "You heard the words Pegasus put into my mouth, Carol honey. *'Carol and I both want you!'*" he repeated softly. "I love you, darlin'. Can't we make Peg's dream come true?"

Carol listened and then she was in his arms. Centaur King held her close and brushed the little tendrils away from her ear with his lips.

"I'm asking you to marry me, Carol," he whispered, and the girl closed her eyes and offered her lips.

"And I love you, Centaur," she whispered. "I didn't know how much until you rode away to meet . . . ?"

286

"I've been thinking," King said softly. "Part of me is a nomad at heart; the other part loves a comfortable home and all that goes with it."

"Love will find a way," Carol answered confidently. "I want you to do just what you want to do . . . always!"

"You do?"

"I do," Carol answered happily.

Centaur King dropped his arms and whispered a warning. "Yonder comes Dapper Jim and the sheriff. Try to act as though nothing unusual has happened!"

"I'll try," Carol promised. "But you have made me the happiest girl in Texas!"

# CHAPTER TWENTY
## PROMISE ME

Pegasus Bronte was in the driver's seat as the Conestoga wagon rolled westward. Centaur King sat beside the boy, making plans for the future, and frowning now and then as his mind dwelled on some doubtful point which might bring up an issue. A week had passed since the capture of Colt Johnson; a happy week during which King had taken long rides with Carol.

Peg handled the long leather lines expertly, and he glanced often at King's face in an effort to read what was going on behind those inscrutable black eyes. The boy coughed a time or two, cleared his throat, and sighed heavily.

"Yeah," King said quietly. "What's on your mind, pard?"

"It's what is on your mind that I can't figure out," Peg Bronte answered honestly. "And I promised to just think about things, and not to blurt out everything like a little old button!"

"You're past being a button now," Centaur King told the boy. "You're seventeen, and doing a man's work. Go ahead, Peg. Speak on out, and I'll answer if I can."

"I love Carol now," the boy said slowly, but

289

with a deep reverence in his eyes. "When are you and Carol going to get married, Centaur?"

King gave a start and looked into the far distance. Then he smiled and spoke slowly.

"We didn't set any date, Peg," he answered. "But we sort of had an understanding that it would be after we finish up here in Stanhope, and before we start for California."

"Where we going to live, Centaur?"

"That's what was worrying me, Peg," King confided. "I've been turning it over in my mind. There's the farm back in the Blue Grass where I was born. It's a lovely old house, and Carol will love it."

Peg Bronte's face clouded. "I was afraid of that, Centaur," he said glumly. "What about that land of ours down in the valley where we are running the hoss-band?"

"We will develop that into a modern horse-spread," King answered enthusiastically. "There's a future in Morgan horses, and in those golden Palominos."

"That's for me," Peg declared. "Can I spend a lot of time there?"

"Sure you can," King agreed. "When you become of age, we will change the papers and make you the boss of that ranch. You want to remember that Carol and Crag Tinsley own the adjoining range, and later on they might want you to take over and run it for them."

"Gee, that's swell, Centaur," Peg Bronte whispered huskily. Then he stared hard at King with a little pucker between his wide eyes. "But what about us travelling?" he asked hesitantly.

Centaur King sighed again. "That's what has been worrying me," he admitted frankly. "I know I can never settle down in one place and just stay put. I'll want to travel ever so often, and I'll want to follow my calling!"

"You mean gentling the wild ones," Peg said with an understanding nod of his head.

"Yeah," King agreed. "I'm a showman, and I will always be!"

"This must be the place Dapper Jim was telling us about," Peg said, and he drove off the road and braked the wagon to a stop near a grove of wild pecan trees. A little stream flowed nearby, and the prairie was knee-deep with fragrant bluestem.

Peg Bronte unspanned the team of bays while King staked the two stallions out to graze. They set up camp and went about the familiar chores, and twilight was closing in when they had finished supper.

Centaur King got out his best saddle and went to work with saddle-soap and neats-foot oil. Peg Bronte followed King's example, but he did not speak of the thing weighing on his young mind. Carol and Centaur had both taught him not to blurt out all he thought, and the question was still unanswered when the two turned in for the night.

They were up at dawn, and Peg Bronte watched as King gave the two stallions a generous measure of grain. After breakfast, Centaur King brushed Major Domo thoroughly, rubbed the glistening black coat with an oiled cloth, and then went to the wagon. Peg watched as King brought out a drum and tightened the skin heads. His heart leaped when King brought out a second drum and made the necessary adjustments.

Peg Bronte was bursting with curiosity, but he maintained his silence. His eyes followed Centaur King about, and finally the horse tamer threw back his head and laughed joyously.

"You're learning fast, Pegasus," King praised. "Now you polish up that golden stallion until he shines like pure gold. You and me will double up to-day, even if we never do it again!"

"You mean I'm to beat the skins and have Gold 'Un prance at my heels?" Peg shouted, and then he leaped into the air and cracked his heels together. A moment later his face grew sober, and he came close to King. "You're not going to beat the skins after to-day?" he asked in a shaky whisper.

"I don't know," King answered heavily. "I really don't know."

"She can't do this to us, Centaur!" Peg burst out resentfully.

"That will do, Pegasus!" King admonished

292

sternly. "Now you get busy with your horse and gear. Remember all I've taught you, and don't make any mistakes!"

"You're making one," Peg Bronte muttered just above his breath.

"What's that?" King asked sharply.

"Nothing," Peg growled. "I just sotter slipped and got to thinking out loud again. I'll shine up my hoss!"

Centaur King smiled wistfully as he turned away. He fitted the light head-stall on Major Domo, worked the black stallion for an hour to perfect his routine, and then changed to his best suit of clothes. Peg Bronte was ready when King came from the wagon, and the boy was perfectly groomed. He had discarded his dinky hat for a new grey Stetson, and the golden stallion glistened in the early morning sun.

King picked up his drum and slipped the lanyard around his neck and under the collar of his coat. He smiled with his lips when Peg Bronte copied his every move. King turned with the drumsticks in his right hand.

"It's a bit more than a mile to Stanhope," he told the boy. "You keep twenty paces behind Major Domo, and see that you control your horse. We've got to put on a good show, and mind you keep your eyes front and centre!"

"Like you said, Centaur," Peg answered quietly, and only his dark eyes betrayed the excitement he felt. For the first time he was going to beat the skins with a stallion prancing behind him. He watched Centaur King who slipped the loop from Major Domo's right foreleg, and Peg Bronte took his place beside the golden stallion.

King walked out in front of his horse, poised his drumsticks, and then began to beat a tattoo. Major Domo raised his head and reared high in the air. King began to march without a backward glance, and the black stallion followed like a well-trained dog.

Pegasus Bronte judged the distance and spoke softly to Golden. "Do me right, Gold 'Un," the boy pleaded. "We got to make good for the master!"

His sticks came down and struck the tight drumhead in perfect time with the roll of King's ratapan. Golden reared high and began to prance. Then he followed the slender boy at ten paces, and the triumphal march into Stanhope was under way.

Centaur King turned his head slightly to listen to the cadence of Peg Bronte's flashing sticks. The older man smiled with satisfaction as he could detect no echo. The two drums might have been played by the same hands, and King changed the rhythm and started a single beat like a signalling tom-tom.

Peg Bronte knew the change was coming, and he also knew that the message of the two drums could be heard in the town down the winding road. King switched to a marching routine which they maintained until they came within sight of the store-fronts down in Stanhope.

Now the drums increased the cadence and began to vibrate under the difficult double roll. The two stallions showed excitement and began to prance. Then Centaur King passed the first curious spectators, but he looked neither to the right nor left.

Now they were in the centre of the thriving little town, and both sidewalks were lined with interested residents. Centaur King glanced up at a cloth banner stretched across the street from curb to curb, and his dark eyes widened. The banner bore a sign in large letters which read:

"STANHOPE WELCOMES CENTAUR KING AND PEGASUS BRONTE!"

King knew that Peg had seen the welcome when the boy faltered and missed a beat. Peg Bronte recovered instantly, and he beat his drum proudly as the golden stallion pranced and curvetted just ten paces behind him.

Centaur King saw the sales ring over to the right, and he made a smart right turn. Now his hands were flashing as he executed a broken routine which sounded like long dots and short dashes. He walked proudly into the show ring with Major Domo at his heels, and Peg Bronte followed through like a veteran. The drums came to a silence which beat down upon the ears, and the horse tamers turned and slipped the loops over forelegs in perfect unison.

A man mounted the platform on the auction block. Centaur King smiled when he recognized the checkered cut-away coat of Dapper Jim Stacey. His eyes widened when he saw Sheriff Ben Clay standing with a familiar figure, and King recognized the marshal of Lanthrope.

But Crag Tinsley was not alone. Rose Tinsley and little Madeline sat in the seat of honour with the marshal, and then King saw Carol. She was wearing a new riding outfit of divided leather skirt with a bolero jacket, and her heavy silk blouse was open at the neck. Dapper Jim cracked his long whip and cleared his throat.

"Welcome to Stanhope, Centaur King, and Pegasus Bronte!" the auctioneer spoke for the townsfolk. "You two need no introduction here, and we are about to open the monthly sale. Would you cow people like to hear a few words from the greatest horse tamer in the world?"

Cheers answered Jim Stacey, and he waved his hand for silence.

"Once in every hundred years, a man is born who is blessed with . . . *the gift,*'" Stacey said clearly. "He can walk into a corral filled with wild fighting horses, and he can quiet them

296

with a touch of the hand. Ladies and gentlemen of Stanhope, Texas, it is my pleasure to present to you . . . that master horse tamer . . . Centaur King!"

Centaur King bowed from the hips and removed his Stetson. He walked to the platform and studied the bronzed eager faces of the big crowd. He glanced at Carol Tinsley and seemed to hesitate, and then he smiled when Carol nodded with a smile.

"I want to thank you folks for the welcome you have given Peg and me," King began in his slow drawl, but his deep voice was vibrant with happiness. "It is true that I have been blessed with the gift, but there is one other who has this same treasure. He will be a master of horses in his own right, my young partner . . . Pegasus Bronte!"

Peg Bronte uncovered and bowed from the hips. The two beautiful stallions stood immovable, and Centaur King began to speak again.

"We do not mean to interfere with the work of the regular horse-breakers," he said clearly. "But if you have any animals you cannot handle, or any who are downright vicious, we will guarantee to correct these faults. We will stay here in Stanhope for two weeks, and I ask you to do us a favour. Bring us wild horses!"

Centaur King bowed again and walked back to Major Domo. He unfastened the loop and walked behind the ring, and the black stallion followed quietly. Pegasus Bronte took his bow, unfastened his loop, and Golden followed the boy like a great docile dog.

King turned his horse into an empty pen, and watched while Peg Bronte performed a similar service for Golden. Peg said he would stay with the stallions while the sale was in progress, and Centaur King slapped the boy heartily between the shoulders.

"You behaved like an old trouper, Peg!" he praised warmly. "And you had Golden working perfectly."

"I'm so dad-burned happy I'm about to bust!" Pegasus said with a sigh. "Me a-beatin' the skins with a golden stud prancin' and a-faunchin' at my heels. Centaur, I'd want to die if we had to quit puttin' on our show!"

"You won't ever have to quit, Peg," a throaty voice said in a husky whisper.

Centaur King and the boy whirled to face Carol Tinsley. Little Madeline ran to Peg Bronte and held out her arms. Peg picked her up, and Madeline puckered her lips.

"Kiss your Sugar Foots, Peggie!" she ordered imperiously.

Peg kissed the child and hugged her close. Then his face clouded as he began to scold. "You don't stop callin' me Peggie, I aim to do you a meanness!" he threatened crossly.

"You don't love me no more!" Madeline wailed, and Peg Bronte gave up the fight.

"Sure I do, Sugar Foots," he said hastily. "Ole Peggie will always love you, you ornery little ole jughead!"

Centaur King smiled as Carol took his arm. She led him away to a clump of trees near a big barn, and King walked proudly at her side. Carol was radiant with happiness, and her pretty face was alive with vivid colouring.

"Please don't worry any more, Centaur," she pleaded. "I was so proud of you when you came down the street with Major Domo prancing at your heels. Something fine and sincere would go out of your life if you ever gave it up, and I want you to promise me that you never will!"

Centaur King stepped back and stared at the pretty girl. His lips parted to show his even white teeth, and then a happy smile drove the lines of worry from his dark, handsome face.

"You mean . . . you mean you want me to continue beating the skins?" he whispered. "You say you won't object to me putting on a show when we come to a new town?"

"Object?" Carol echoed. "I won't marry you if you change one little bit, Centaur King!"

"Well, dad-burn my hide!" Centaur King whispered, and then he leaped high in the air and cracked the heels of his polished cowboy boots together like a boy.

The next instant he had Carol in his strong arms, holding her close, with his lips close to the tendrils which curled around her small ears.

"I love you, darlin'," he whispered tenderly. "I've wandered over most of the world, seeking for just one thing, and now I've found it!"

"You mean . . . happiness and content?" Carol asked in a tremulous whisper.

"Happiness, contentment, and love," Centaur King answered humbly.

Carol raised her head from the shelter of his shoulder. She looked deeply into his expressive dark eyes, and then she offered her lips.

"I love you, Centaur," she said softly. "I'll never want you to be any different."

Centaur King kissed her hungrily as he tightened his arms. Much later he sighed and held her away as he searched her face.

"Pegasus," he said wistfully. "He's my partner!"

"He isn't," Carol contradicted. "Pegasus is *our* partner. I won't have it any other way. He loves the open road as much as you and I, and Peg made me promise to go along with you all to California. I will paint some wonderful pictures, but I won't go unless Peg goes with us!"

"Sugar," Centaur King murmured, and once more he tightened his arms. "And when we go to Kentucky to live part of the time?" he whispered.

"I'll love it, but not unless Peg comes along," Carol said firmly. "I love that boy, Centaur. It isn't every girl who has two fine men to love!"

"I feel just like Pegasus did just before you came around back," King said with a little smile curling his full lips. "I feel so dad-burned happy I could bust!"

"There's just one other thing," Carol said gently.

"Name it!" King answered promptly. "And I'll either do it, or have it done!"

"The gift," Carol whispered, and her eyes reflected the awe she felt in her heart. "The gift is given only once in a century. You'll always use it, Centaur!"

"I will!" Centaur King promised humbly. "You heard what I told the folks a while ago, and now I can keep on telling them wherever we go. Perhaps we better go back there now and remind 'em again. After I tell them that you and I are going to be married to-morrow. I'll ask them again to . . . Bring me Wild Horses!"

**Center Point Large Print**
600 Brooks Road / PO Box 1
Thorndike, ME 04986-0001 USA

(207) 568-3717

**US & Canada:**
**1 800 929-9108**
www.centerpointlargeprint.com